Shadows and Lies

A World of Gothic · United States

RAINE ENGLISH

Elusive Dreams Press

Shadows and Lies: A World of Gothic: United States

Contact information:
publisher@elusivedreamspress.com

Cover Art by *Elusive Dreams Designs*

Elusive Dreams Press
PO Box 2024
North Haven, CT 06473

Visit us at www.ElusiveDreamsPress.com

Electronic ISBN: 978-1-62935-041-7
Print ISBN: 978-1-62935-042-4

Published in the United States of America

A shadowy figure haunts Turnberry House

As I stood looking at the house, clouds covered the sun, darkening the bright, beautiful day and casting shadows over Turnberry, giving it a much more sinister appearance. My gaze traveled up to the second floor, and I could have sworn I saw someone staring out from one of the large paned windows, but upon second glance, no one was there. Could it have been my imagination, or had someone been watching me arrive?

My fingers curled around the spinel pendant that hung from my neck, and I stroked the cool, smooth stone, hoping it would help to ease my anxiety.

"That's a lovely necklace, Miss Oliva," Gerard said, his gaze fixed on the pendant.

"Thank you. My mother gave it to me."

"Many people confuse spinel with rubies, but I don't quite know how that's possible. No other stone gives off that fire. Did you know it has mystic qualities?"

I nodded, thinking back to how my mother had said it would protect me...

———————————

To Mom, for always believing in me.

Prologue

Turnberry House Plantation - Louisiana, 1831

THE STALE AIR in the tiny room smelled of mold, and I fought hard to keep from gaging. One would think there was no way the three of us could've fit in this little space. Yet, somehow we had. None too comfortably, though, I might add. The heel of Nathan's shoe pushed into the toe of my boot and I wanted to cry out in pain, but if I did, I'd be placing us all in jeopardy. Instead, I bit my lip—so hard I tasted blood.

Small, thin fingers curled around my hand. I squinted, trying to make out Mary's face. However, the room was as black as a moonless September night. It didn't matter that I couldn't see her, though. We were all in this together now... And if our plan didn't work, we'd die together too. I sucked in a deep breath and tried to push that horrid thought from my mind.

Something crawled across the top of my head. I envisioned a spider—big and black and furry. I hated the creatures, and it took all my courage not to scream. I don't know how I was able to muster the strength—maybe it was because I imagined the thing crawling down onto my face—but I reached up with my other hand and swiped it off.

Relief ran through me, but that was quickly replaced with heart thundering fear at the sound of voices outside the door. As they neared our hiding place, my body recoiled, and I instinctively pushed my back harder up against the wall.

"They gotta be here somewhere." I recognized the low, thick voice as Tucker Sheldon's, manager at Clairmont Plantation. He was as mean as a grizzly bear.

Next came what sounded like the tapping of a cane across the hardwood floor. Samuel Clairmont used a cane! My stomach clenched tight. That man would stop at nothing to get what he wanted.

"Well, you better find them..." His refined voice

trailed off, and I imagined his bushy white brows drawn together in anger. He was an impatient man, one who took swift and harsh action against all who crossed him. A shiver of panic ran down the back of my neck at the thought of what he would do to us if discovered.

I imagined the old man's stale whiskey breath against my face as he yanked me out of my hideaway, his full lips turned up and his small dark eyes glinting with pleasure as he snarled, "You're going to pay dearly for what you did."

My thoughts were brought back to the present by the sound of Sarah Turnberry's sweet, lilting voice. "I told you they weren't here. My heavens, why in the world would they be hidin' in my bedroom, of all places?"

"They might think they're clever," old man Clairmont snarled. "But they're not so clever as to outsmart me. I will find them, and when I do, they'll be sorry they were ever born."

Footsteps crossed the room, stopping just outside the closet, and then I heard the rustling of gowns that covered the entryway to our hiding place. "All this searchin' has made me hot and parched. So if you'll excuse me, I'm goin' to change into somethin' cooler and then go down to the parlor for some punch," Sarah said.

"I'll tell Ellen to bring a pitcher and some cakes, as well." The deep, masculine voice had a huskiness to its tone. Ellis Clairmont was nothing like his father. He was kind and loving.

My thoughts drifted back to last night when the two of us had stood behind the wide trunk of an old cypress tree, stealing kisses in the moonlight. I remembered the feel of his strong hands on my skin. No one had ever made me feel the way Ellis did.

"Darlin', you really are the most considerate man I've ever met." Sarah's voice broke through my reverie.

"Don't be too long," Ellis replied. "We have weddin' plans to go over. If you want to be married by Christmas, there's no time to waste."

Married? In three months? My mouth went dry. It felt like someone had sucked all the air out of the room. I struggled to catch my breath, but that was impossible with my racing heart.

I clasped the red spinel pendant that hung from the necklace I wore. Madame Tousseau had given it to me the last time she'd read my cards.

She'd said it would protect me from danger. I never expected the danger to come from man I loved, though... But if he lied about us, what else was he capable of? I'd told him some of my darkest secrets. Secrets that not only affected me, but Mary and Nathan too. I began to shake as fear swept through me. A moment later the world seemed to slip away and that's the last thing I remembered.

Chapter One

Present Day – Boston, Massachusetts

"OLIVIA LOCKWOOD! WERE you really going to leave town without telling me?"

I slapped my menu shut and placed it on the table in front of me as Kelly Ryan plopped into the booth across from me. The perky blonde stared at me with hands planted on hips.

"We graduated two weeks ago, and news still travels through the grapevine at lightning speed," I replied.

"Yep! Well, I pay special attention to gossip when it concerns my best friend."

I looked away from her probing eyes and shifted my gaze to one of the many TVs plastered around the Pineapple Cantina, but Kelly wasn't about to let me off the hook that easily.

"Is it true you're moving to New Orleans, the most haunted city in the country? I'm so jealous. Guess I'll be visiting often."

I rolled my eyes but couldn't help laughing either. Kelly had a flair for the dramatic that I always found quite amusing. We were complete opposites. Maybe that was why we got along so well. She was an outgoing party girl, while I was more of a loner who had a head for numbers.

"I'm not going to New Orleans. I'm going to Kaylene—about fifty miles west of the city. And I'm not moving there. I'm just going to visit my grandfather."

"So you will be coming back?"

"Of course. Why wouldn't I?"

"Coming back from where?" Dale Ross slid next to me in the booth and draped his arm across my shoulders.

Kelly raised one thin brow. "So you didn't tell him either?"

I struggled to find the right words to explain why I'd put off breaking the news to them, but my mouth felt as dry as sawdust. I took a long drink of ice water and was glad that the waitress chose this moment to come over to take our order. "I'll have the veggie burger and curly fries," I said, happy for the distraction.

"And I'll get a cheeseburger and regular fries." Dale quickly gathered up both menus and handed them to the server.

"I'm not eating," Kelly said. "Just visiting before my friend here goes to Louisiana, and I might never see her again."

When the waitress walked away, I shot Kelly a dirty look, but I might not have bothered because it did nothing to deter her. "Livvy's going to her grandfather's old sugar plantation. I guess telling us that she was leaving was a last-minute annoyance."

I puckered my lips in frustration. "Very funny, Kel. You know that's not true. I put it off because you guys *are* that important to me. It's not like I want to go there. In fact, I've been trying to find an excuse not to, but I haven't been able to come up with one."

"Can't you say you just got your dream job and aren't able to take time off?" she asked.

I took another drink of water and swallowed hard. "My grandfather's dying."

Dale pulled me closer to him. "I'm so sorry, Liv."

"Me too. You know you have to go, girl," Kelly replied in a low voice.

A deep pain stabbed at my heart. A vision of my mother's frail body and pallid face entered my mind's eye. She'd looked so small and helpless lying in that big old four-poster bed, yet still beautiful even while near death. According to my dad, I was the spitting image of her, and although I do have the same straight dark hair and periwinkle eyes, I would never go so far as to call myself beautiful.

"I haven't been there in years. Not since my mom got sick...and the memories are really painful. I'm not sure how I'll react going back to that place."

"It's always more tragic losing a parent when you're a kid, but maybe now that you're an adult, you can take all that hurt and turn it into something productive." Dale kissed me softly.

"Hearing your practical advice is one of the things I love most about you."

"Kelly, did you hear that? I think Livvy used the word love." Dale beamed.

"I heard it. Loud and clear." Kelly chuckled.

It was no secret that Dale wanted us to have a

serious relationship, but I wasn't ready for that. I had so much I needed to figure out, like what I wanted to do with my life. Thinking about marriage right now was not on my to-do list. Besides, deep down, I wanted that heart-pounding, pulse-racing, spine-tingling, rock-my-world kind of feeling. And that just wasn't there with Dale. But the guy who would give me that was out there somewhere, and someday I would find him. "Come on, you guys. You know I love you both."

Although they each nodded, I could see in Dale's eyes that he knew I didn't mean it in the way he'd hoped.

"How long will you be gone?" he asked, twisting a strand of my hair between his fingertips.

I shrugged. "I don't know. As long as it takes. My grandfather's estate manager sent me an email saying I needed to come right away. Grandfather was insisting he'd never rest peacefully if he didn't get to see me."

"When are you leaving?" His tone was solemn.

I hesitated a moment before blurting out, "Day after tomorrow."

The hurt look in his eyes broke my heart, so I glanced down at my hands clenched tightly in my lap. "I'm sorry for not telling you sooner."

"You don't need to be sorry. Just do what you have to do. You know I'll be here when you get back."

"Thanks. I appreciate that." There were so many times I wished I could make myself feel more for Dale. But no matter how hard I tried, I couldn't make my heart flutter the way I wanted it to when I was around him. He was hot, kind, and considerate. Everything a girl could want. Maybe that magical feeling would come with time, and then I'd discover that he was the rock-my-world guy I wanted... Maybe being away from him was what was needed to make that happen... Guess I was about to find out.

"Do you think your grandfather's house is haunted?" Kelly asked, shifting my thoughts away from my lack of romantic feelings for Dale.

I made a face at her. "You know I don't believe in stuff like that."

Undaunted, she went on to say, "I remember you told me once that the plantation was built in the 1790s. Being that old, there are bound to be some ghosts in the place. I'll bet by the time you come back, you'll be a believer. I hope the spirits that are there aren't evil ones, though—out for revenge or possession."

Luckily, the waitress came by with our food at the perfect time, ending Kelly's talk of the paranormal. While we ate, Dale told us about the apartment he found in Allston.

"You'll love it, Liv. It's on the first floor, has two bedrooms, lots of windows. I was hoping to show it to you tomorrow before I sign the lease."

I forced a smile. I know he was hoping I'd want to move in, even though I'd told him many times that I couldn't afford an apartment right now. "Oh, Dale, I've got so much packing and stuff to do before I leave... I just don't know how I'd find the time. I'm sure it's lovely...and if you like it, that's all that matters."

A glazed look of despair spread over his face, but he tried to hide it by saying, "Sure. I understand. You'll see it when you get back."

We stayed at the Pineapple for about another hour, reminiscing about fun times at school, and before leaving, they wished me a quick and safe trip back.

Outside the restaurant, I gave them both a hug before hopping on the T that would take me to

Beacon Street and the old brownstone where I lived with my dad.

He was sitting in the living room reading the *Globe* when I came in. "Hey, there Livvy Luv," he said, glancing over the top of the paper, his reading glasses resting on the end of his nose. "You ready for your trip?"

I shook my head. "Not even close. I need to pack. But before that, I have to decide what to bring. I better get going on that, huh?"

"Probably be a good idea. Have you had dinner? There are leftovers in the fridge."

"I ate at the Pineapple. Said good-bye to Dale and Kelly."

"They're going to miss you, but not near as much as I will."

"It's not too late for you to come with me," I replied, wishing he'd change his mind about going to Louisiana. But even as I said it, I knew there was little chance of that, and not just because it would be tough for him to take time off from his law practice. His memories of Turnberry were even more difficult to deal with than mine—he'd lost his wife there. What should have been a happy family vacation turned into the saddest time of our lives.

My mother had left Boston a vibrant, healthy woman, and within a week, she was bedridden, and then shortly after that, gone. I was too young to remember the details, having been only ten years old—just that the cause of my mom's death had been undetermined—most likely some kind of flu—but I was sure they were etched like stone into my father's mind.

"You know I can't," he said sadly.

I crossed the room to kiss his cheek. "I know. And I'll miss you bunches too. But I won't be long. Promise."

He let the paper drop onto his lap and hugged me. "Make sure you take care of yourself while you're there."

I felt his shoulders sag and knew exactly what he meant. I was all he had. "Don't worry, Dad. I will. And I'll be back before you know it."

There were tears in his eyes. "Go on, go pack," he ordered, obviously embarrassed by his show of emotion.

I squeezed his hand, then left the room and headed upstairs to my bedroom, where I pulled my suitcase out from the back of the closet.

I didn't pay much attention to what I packed.

My thoughts were scattered, jumping from one thing to the next. Putting my life on hold, and that included my career, was not what I wanted to do, but what choice did I have? I might not remember my grandfather well, but he was still my grandfather. How could I refuse his dying wish?

I threw a few more T-shirts into the suitcase before sitting on top of it so that I could get it zipped. I wasn't much of a traveler, and I certainly wasn't a light packer.

The only things left to take were my toiletries and jewelry. I walked over to my armoire and lifted the lid, taking out my two favorite rings, a gold bangle bracelet, and a pair of hoop earrings, then I opened a small drawer. I sucked in my breath as I looked at the vibrant flame-red spinel pendant. Two carats of neon-like fluorescence glowed to such an extent that the stone looked like it was shooting off sparks.

My hands trembled as I lifted the pendant from the box and placed it around my neck. Almost immediately, a sense of calm fell over me, and all the day's stresses melted away.

My mother had given it me, and it was the only thing I owned that had belonged to her. I never wore it. I cherished it too much and was afraid of losing it. My mom had said it would protect me from danger. Having grown up near New Orleans, she'd believed in the metaphysical. And even though I didn't, for some reason I felt compelled to take it with me to Louisiana. Maybe it was due to Kelly's talk of ghosts or my dad's request that I take care of myself. Whatever it was, I planned to heed this strange sense of foreboding. I'd be wearing the necklace to Turnberry.

Chapter Two

Present Day – Louisiana

BEADS OF PERSPIRATION lined my forehead and upper lip. It was a hot, sultry June day in Louisiana, and the hour long ride from New Orleans International Airport to Kaylene in a taxi without air-conditioning made it even more uncomfortable. As we drove along River Road, or what many call Plantation Alley, my gaze scanned broad cane fields and antebellum mansions.

When we approached Turnberry Plantation, the first thing I noticed were the giant oak trees dripping with Spanish moss that lined the long driveway. We drove through the open wrought iron entrance gates, and a minute later, I spotted the massive white mansion built in the Greek Revival style. Its pillars rose to the roofline, and a two-story colonnade surrounded the house. It looked very much like I remembered, only a little more run-down, with its cracked and peeling paint.

Before I'd even gotten out of the taxi, the front door opened and a middle-aged man dressed in a navy suit came out and walked toward the car. He opened my door, and then offered his hand to help me out.

I accepted his assistance, stepping onto the driveway with as much grace as I could manage after a long day of traveling.

"Good afternoon, Miss Olivia. I'm Gerard, your grandfather's butler. It's a pleasure to meet you."

"Thank you. It's nice to meet you too." When I started to rummage through my purse for money to pay the taxi driver, Gerard reached into his pocket and pulled out a wad of bills. I opened my mouth to protest, but he held up his hand, silencing me.

"Don't be silly. Your grandfather invited you here. He doesn't expect you to pay for anything."

I raised my brows in surprise. Grandfather had paid for my plane fare, but I certainly never expected that he would pay for more than that. A moment later, my bags were taken out of the trunk, after which the taxi quickly drove away.

As I stood looking at the house, clouds covered the sun, darkening the bright, beautiful day and casting shadows over Turnberry, giving it a much more sinister appearance. My gaze traveled up to the second floor, and I could have sworn I saw someone staring out from one of the large paned windows, but upon second glance, no one was there. Could it have been my imagination, or had someone been watching me arrive?

My fingers curled around the spinel pendant that hung from my neck, and I stroked the cool, smooth stone, hoping it would help to ease my anxiety.

"That's a lovely necklace, Miss Olivia," Gerard said, his gaze fixed on the pendant.

"Thank you. My mother gave it to me."

"Many people confuse spinel with rubies, but I don't quite know how that's possible. No other stone gives off that fire. Did you know it has mystic qualities?"

I nodded, thinking back to how my mother had said it would protect me, but not wanting to mention that. I grabbed my backpack, Gerard took my suitcase, and together we walked toward the front door.

The vestibule had an eerie quality. Although spectacular with its black-and-white marble floor and curved mahogany-railed staircase, the house was dark and badly in need of a new coat of paint. The antique furniture made me feel like I'd gone back to another era. And despite what was still a beautiful home, the place seemed sad, as if all the life had been drained from it.

"Follow me," Gerard said, heading up the staircase. "I'll show you to your room. I'm sure you'll want to freshen up after your trip and before seeing your grandfather."

"Yes, thank you. You read my mind."

He stopped halfway down the narrow, dark hall and opened the door to one of the many guest rooms. Decorated with splashes of pink and white and green, it was prettier than I'd expected, despite needing to have the yellowed wallpaper removed. I imagined a number of Southern belles had stayed here throughout the years, while attending parties or balls.

Gerard set my suitcase down next to the large canopy bed and said, "Tea will be served in the parlor in thirty minutes."

I smiled at him. "That sounds wonderful. Thanks." After he left, I plopped my backpack on the bed and took out my laptop, wondering what the chances were this place had Wi-Fi. I'd have to find out about that.

I kicked off my shoes and then headed into the bathroom to take a quick shower. The cool water felt good on my perspiration-soaked skin, and I closed my eyes, letting it stream over my face and head. Within a few minutes, I was invigorated, and my curiosity mounted as I tried to imagine why my grandfather had invited me here.

After slipping into khakis and a white tee, I partially dried my hair, then pulled it back into a ponytail. A little lip gloss and mascara were next, and then I was ready to see what fate had in store for me.

When I entered the parlor, I was surprised to find other people there. I immediately recognized my Uncle Paul—my mom's younger brother. The last time I'd seen him was at her funeral. He looked the same, only with grayer hair and a few wrinkles. The woman standing beside him I assumed to be his daughter, Jessica. We used to play together as children whenever my family would come here to visit. Back then, she'd been bossy, using our age difference—she was three years older—to her advantage. The stunning, willowy blonde looked me up and down with her catlike green eyes, and I knew she hadn't changed.

I wasn't about to let her intimidate me, though, as she had when we were young, so with my head held high, I strolled across the room and gave them each a hug. "It's so nice to see you both," I said warmly, thinking I would like to get to know them. Having some other relatives to call family would be a welcome change. It had been just my dad and me for such a long time.

However, my embrace was returned stiffly by each of them. Apparently, they weren't as happy to see me as I was them. Before I had the chance to further ponder their strange reaction to me, a tall, well-muscled man entered the room. He carried himself with a commanding air of self-confidence, and why not? He was ruggedly handsome, with bronzed skin, tawny hair, high cheekbones, and a full, sensuous mouth. The shadow of his beard only added to his powerful, manly aura.

When his gaze landed on Jessica, he smiled,

revealing even, white teeth. But when he looked at me, that smile disappeared, and his blue-gray eyes grew cold as shards of ice. As he studied my face, I stared back at him, and if I didn't know better, I'd say I'd met him before. But that was impossible. Surely, I wouldn't forget someone that handsome. Still, I had the distinct feeling that I knew him, and for a moment, I wondered if he felt the same.

His gaze shifted down to my necklace and the spinel pendant. As it lingered there, his square jaw visibly tensed, then he quickly looked over at my uncle.

"Hello, Paul. Nice to see you again. And you too, Jess." His voice was velvet-edged and strong. He shook their hands, then reached for mine.

His fingers were cool and smooth. "It's a pleasure to meet you Olivia. I'm Jaxon Carter."

My grandfather's estate manager and the man who'd sent me the email asking me to come here? I'd envisioned him as a stocky, balding man in his sixties. Boy, I couldn't have been more wrong!

"I'm pleased to meet you too." I tried to sound nonchalant, not wanting my burning cheeks to make it apparent that his nearness was sending a tingling to the pit of my stomach.

Luckily, a young woman arrived carrying a tray with sweet tea and cucumber finger sandwiches. She handed me a glass, and I quickly took a sip, hoping the cool beverage would tone down my flushed face.

"I hope you had a pleasant trip here," Jaxon said before taking a drink of the delicious tea himself and then a bite of one of the sandwiches.

"Yes, there were no travel issues." I wasn't about to tell him I was a sweaty mess when I arrived due to the taxi not having air-conditioning.

I could feel Jessica's heated stare fixed on me, and when I looked over at her, she made no attempt to look away. Instead, she seemed to challenge me, as if to say I was infringing on her territory. Well, she didn't have to worry. I wasn't planning on staying at Turnberry long.

I opened my mouth to say something to her, but snapped it shut when my grandfather arrived, being pushed in a wheelchair by Gerard. Although in his mid-seventies, he looked much older than that. He'd always been a robust man. That was not the case now. Thin and wizened, Asa was a far cry from the man I remembered. His skin had numerous irritations, and along with his thinning hair, there were bald spots. Yet, despite the physical changes, his warm personality remained. "Livvy, my dear, I can't believe you're really here."

He opened his arms to me, and I went willingly into them. "It's so great to see you again, Grandpa." I kissed his cheek, and when I leaned back to look at him, his eyes were moist with tears.

"You look just like your mother, my beautiful, sweet Ann." As he said those words, a faraway look came over his face, and my heart went out to him. None of us were the same after my mom's death, but it seemed Asa might have been affected the most. My father had told me that for years, Grandfather refused to let anyone in my mother's room, not even to clean it. And he'd become so despondent that last year, he stopped producing sugarcane—laid off the workers and just completely shut down the plantation. The only people he kept on were the house workers. It was shortly after that that he became ill, apparently giving up on life.

I hoped my being here would do him some good. "I miss her too," I whispered against his cheek. "Every day."

That seemed to soothe him some, knowing that he wasn't alone in his misery. He patted my hands, then turned to Uncle Paul and Jessica. "I'm glad you two are here as well, but not for the same reason."

Both my uncle and cousin noticeably stiffened, and their faces went pale. There was no doubt my grandfather's words were meant to be insulting, and the tension in the room ramped up a notch. I had no idea what was going on between them, but I had a pretty good idea I was about to find out.

Chapter Three

EVERYONE SEEMED TO have relaxed a little as we ate cucumber finger sandwiches, sipped on sweet tea, and chatted about nonconfrontational subjects, such as my Environmental Science major. They all seemed interested in college life, and I was able to entertain them with stories of my time at school.

However, the atmosphere changed again when Grandfather brought up the reason we were here. "William Turnberry built this house. It was smaller then, and Creole in style. It wasn't until 1830 that it was enlarged to its current size and renovated to a Greek Revival. It's always belonged to a Turnberry, except for a short time when Union soldiers took it over during the Civil War, but it was given back to us. And I'm going to make sure it continues to stay in the family." His voice was strong and clear and determined.

We all were familiar with the plantation's history, and I could tell by the looks on everyone's faces that they were wondering about the purpose for Asa's monologue. He didn't keep us in suspense much longer.

"I asked you all here today," he went on to say, "because I know my days are numbered, and I want to be sure that my wishes are adhered to. I don't want anyone disputing my will; therefore, you're going to hear what's in it today."

Uncle Paul let out an audible gasp. "Dad, you can't be serious. That's beyond morbid."

Asa laughed. "It's too late to pretend that you give a hoot about me. You should have thought about that years ago."

Paul's face turned red, and he started to protest, but Grandfather held up his hand, silencing him.

"This isn't open to debate. My witnesses are here: Jaxon, Gerard, and Theresa." Asa looked over at the young woman cleaning up our sandwich dishes. "You're all to note that I'm of sound mind and judgment, and no one has coerced me into anything."

The three of them agreed.

"It's no secret that I loved Ann very much, and it's almost time for me to be reunited with her. But before I leave this earth, I want to honor her life by granting her fondest wish—to turn this place into a bed-and-breakfast and let people from all over experience a little bit of the history that this property has to offer. I don't want it sold off to the highest bidder or largest petrochemical plant."

He paused for a moment and directed his gaze at me. "So on behalf of your wonderful mother, I leave to you, Livvy, the plantation and all of its assets. In addition, eighty percent of my fortune will go to you. I don't have the exact amount. Who can keep track of such things? Jaxon can get that for you."

My hand flew up to my mouth, and my eyes grew wide with disbelief. As I scanned the room, I saw that everyone else appeared shocked too. Uncle Paul looked furious, and Jessica was as white as a ghost.

Grandfather clearly hadn't missed their reactions either, because he said, "Don't worry, you two. You'll each get ten percent. That'll give you enough to live comfortably for the rest of your lives. And if that doesn't make you happy, too bad. Go find a job."

Before anyone could speak, he added, "And one more thing. Livvy, I know this is a lot for you to take in. I don't expect you to just up and leave your life in Boston, so I've made your inheritance contingent upon you living here and running the bed-and-breakfast for six months. After that time, if you want to go back to your old life, you may do so and keep the money you've inherited. The plantation, though, will be given to the Kaylene Historical Society. However, if you don't fulfill that six-month promise, you'll receive nothing."

As I stood frozen with shock, I noticed my uncle's face brighten some. Jessica was still as washed-out as before, though, and Jaxon, who was leaning up against the fireplace mantel, seemed to be measuring us all with a cool, appraising look.

Theresa piled the rest of the dishes onto the tray. "Mr. Turnberry, if ya don't need me for anythin' else, I'm goin' to go back to the kitchen. I have to help Dottie prepare tonight's dinner."

Grandfather smiled at the little redheaded girl. "Of course, of course. And thank you for witnessing my will."

She quickly left the room, shifting all attention back to me. My mind was still swirling as I tried to comprehend what had just transpired. I knew my grandfather was waiting for some kind of response from me, but I had no idea what to say. How in the world could I accept his proposal? I didn't even want to come here to visit, let alone remain for six months. He was right about one thing. My life *was* in Boston, and that was how I wanted it to stay. Besides, I knew nothing about the running of a bed-and-breakfast. Yet, something tugged at my heart and the memory of my mother's sweet face filled my mind. How could I not honor her dream?

I never liked making difficult decisions, and this one was extremely hard. There was lots to consider, and it would take some time for me to make up my mind.

I cleared my throat before speaking. "While this offer is extremely generous, Grandpa, I hope you don't mind if I don't give you an answer right now...today."

He waved for me to come over and stand beside him. When I did, he took hold of my hand and squeezed it. "I didn't expect an answer today, my dear. Take some time. Just not too much. An answer tomorrow will be fine." He took a deep breath and began to cough.

It was evident the uncertainty of what I would do was stressful for him. "Will it be all right if I let you know in the morning?"

His faded eyes brightened some. "That'll be just wonderful." With that said, he motioned for Gerard, who'd been sitting by the large, paned window. "I'm going to rest now. I'll see you all at dinner."

After he left the room, Uncle Paul said, "Jess, do you still want to spend the night, or would you rather go back to New Orleans now?"

Awkwardly, she said, "I'd rather leave in the morning."

"Fine," Uncle Paul snapped, making no attempt to cover his annoyance. "Jaxon, would you have someone bring the car around? I'm going for a drive."

His blue-gray eyes were hooded, so I couldn't read his expression. But as Jaxon walked past Jessica, she said something to him under her breath, and he nodded in agreement. From the way he'd smiled at her earlier and by the look on her face now, I wondered if there was something going on between them. And why not? They were both very good-looking. I could see where they'd have at least a strong physical connection. Yet, for some odd reason, I found that thought extremely distasteful.

"I'll see you later." Uncle Paul kissed my cheek.

"My head is pounding. I'm going up to my room to lay down for a while. We'll catch up later," Jess said to me.

"Feel better soon," I replied.

A moment later, I found myself alone in the parlor and with an overwhelming need for fresh air. I left the house and strolled around back to the French parterre garden. I took my time wandering along the gravel pathways that separated the many planting beds, all consisting of tightly clipped hedging. When I reached the center, I stopped at the fountain, my gaze fixed on a lovely concrete angel spewing water. I concentrated on its relaxing sound, hoping it would bring some much-needed clarity to my jumbled thoughts. How was I going to give Grandfather an answer by morning when I didn't have the slightest idea what to do? I tried to think of the positives and negatives of both scenarios, ruling out the idea of living at Turnberry indefinitely, though. If I stayed the six months, I'd inherit the money, and then I could pay off my student loan debt. That was very appealing. But six months was a long time to put my life in Boston on hold. I certainly couldn't ask Dale to wait that long, nor would I want him to. And what about my dad? How would he cope all that time without me?

With a sigh, I continued my walk, passing through white swinging gates to the area of the plantation where a number of historic buildings still stood, including a pigeonnier, an overseer's cottage, a few barns, a sugar house, and a couple of slave quarters. I headed over to one, and on my way, I heard voices coming from behind a cypress tree. There was no mistaking the female as Jessica.

"I can't believe my grandfather would do that to me," she whined. "I've been visiting him twice a week for months. That should count for something, shouldn't it?"

"I'm sure he appreciates that," Jaxon replied in his sexy drawl.

"How can you say that when he all but left me out of his will?"

"Don't worry. I doubt that city girl could last

two weeks here, let alone six months."

The hairs on the back of my neck bristled at Jaxon's response. He knew nothing about me, yet he assumed I was soft and weak.

Jessica giggled. "I'll bet you're right. Once she's gone, I can work on Grandfather."

Anger boiled inside me, and I couldn't listen to more, afraid I might not be able to keep silent much longer. I raced over to one of the slave quarters and hurried up the rickety steps to the tiny front porch, not caring that I twisted my ankle in the process.

It took a minute for my eyes to adjust to the darkness inside. The room was empty except for an old wooden rocking chair. I sank onto it, rubbing my ankle and trying to calm my racing heart. Guess I'd been as wrong about Jaxon as he'd been about me. Just because he was handsome, polite, and sexy as heck, that didn't make him someone I'd like to get to know better. Besides, he was a terrible judge of character to be involved with someone like Jessica.

I leaned back in the chair, taking in my surroundings. The place was musty and damp and had an air of intense sadness to it. I closed my eyes and thought of all the men and women who'd lived here and how their lives had revolved around milling sugar cane and doing the bidding of their master—hard work in the sugar cane fields from sunrise to sunset. I could almost feel their muscles straining in pain, and a deep, unaccustomed misery tore at my heart.

The door flew open, jolting me from my vision, and I nearly jumped out of my skin when I spotted Jaxon standing there.

"I saw you trip and thought you might be hurt."

I sprang out of the chair and stormed past him. "See," I said, marching down the steps. "I'm fine. Not a weak city girl after all."

His gaze was riveted on me, but before he could say a word, I left him standing in the doorway.

I didn't care that my ankle throbbed. I raced through the white swinging gates and through the French parterre garden, then up the back stairs to the rear porch. When I entered the house, Theresa came hurrying out of the kitchen toward me.

"Miss Olivia, dinner's bein' served in the dinin' room." Wisps of her red hair poked out from beneath her hairnet, and she had traces of flour still on her hands.

"Thank you." I hadn't realized so much time had passed since having tea. I walked through the vestibule and then into the dining room, surprised to find it empty.

I chose a seat at the far end of the table, and while I waited for the others to arrive, I reflected on the events of the day. Earlier, I'd had no idea what to expect and certainly never anticipated having my grandfather want to leave me the plantation. Once again, I thought of my mother and her dream of turning it into a bed-and-breakfast. I glanced around the room and tried to envision it full of guests waiting for dinner. Could I handle the running of a place this size? And did I even want to try? These were questions I couldn't answer. Yet, I had to make a decision by morning.

Chapter Four

I HADN'T HEARD Jaxon come in and wasn't even aware that he was in the dining room until he sat across from me at the table.

"How's your ankle? The way you ran out of that shack, I wouldn't be surprised if you injured it more."

I studied him carefully before answering, trying to determine whether he was mocking me or truly interested in how I was feeling. There was genuine concern on his face, so my hackles went down a little. "It's fine. Just a slight twist. I'm sure it'll be good as new in no time."

"The comment you made before you left, about not being a weak city girl, I take it you said that because you overheard me talking to Jessica."

My cheeks warmed. "I wasn't eavesdropping," I said defensively. "I was taking a walk and just happened to hear you."

He seemed to choose his words carefully. "What I said wasn't meant as an insult. And I never called you weak, by the way. That's something you misinterpreted."

I scowled at him. "Oh, really. How should I have interpreted it, then?"

"I simply meant there's quite a difference between city life and plantation life. Even though Turnberry's no longer producing sugar cane, there's still a lot of land to maintain. To say nothing of what goes into the running of a bed-and-breakfast."

"And how would you know about that?"

"Because my mother manages the neighboring bed-and-breakfast."

I squinted as I stared at him. "Are you related to Jonathon Clairmont?"

He smiled widely as if reveling in my astonishment. "Yes, he's my uncle."

"I'm surprised my grandfather would hire you with the ongoing feud between our two families." I was becoming increasingly uneasy under his scrutiny.

"There might not be any love lost between your grandfather and my uncle, but Asa is smart enough to hire the best and most qualified man for the job."

"Hmmm, you're modest too."

"You can add honest to that list, as well."

Before I could respond, Theresa came in carrying a tray filled with food. She set it down between us, in the center of the table, and then removed the lids from each of the delicious looking platters. "I'll be back soon to see if ya need anythin' else."

As she headed out the door, I said, "Shouldn't we wait for the others to join us?"

"I'm sorry, miss. I was told it was just the two of ya. Your grandfather ain't feelin' well, so he had some soup up in his room. Miss Jessica is lyin' down with a headache, and yar uncle called to say dat he was dinin' out with some friends." She offered me a small smile. "Enjoy yar dinner."

If my stomach wasn't grumbling with hunger and the food didn't smell so fabulous, I would've been tempted to leave and let Jaxon eat alone. But the thought of going to bed hungry just to be spiteful seemed foolish at best.

We filled our plates and then began to eat, but

an uncomfortable silence loomed between us, making it impossible to enjoy the meal.

"How long have you worked for my grandfather?" I asked between bites.

"Almost a year. Asa's a wonderful man. Generous and kind. He'd give the shirt off his back if he thought someone needed it. There aren't many men like him left. These past few months have really been tough on him. His body just seemed to give out. Of course, numerous bouts of pneumonia haven't helped."

It was evident that he truly cared for my grandfather, making my feelings toward him soften a little. "There seems to be some bad blood between him and my Uncle Paul. Any idea what that's about?"

Jaxon stared down at his plate.

"I'm sorry. You don't need to answer if you don't want to. I wasn't looking to gossip. It's just that I barely know my grandfather, yet he wants me to inherit nearly all of his estate, leaving very little to his son and other granddaughter. I can see how they'd be angry and feel cheated."

"You don't need to feel bad for your Uncle Paul. Asa has good reason not to want to leave him much.

He'd just gamble it all away…"

I sucked in my breath. I had no idea Uncle Paul was a gambler. "What about Jess? Is he afraid she might have her father's addiction?"

Jaxon hesitated again, and I could see that this was making him uncomfortable. "I'm sorry. I understand if you don't want to talk about her, you two being involved and all."

"What? Involved like romantically?" His mouth quivered a little, and I could tell he was trying not to laugh.

I frowned. "Why is that funny?"

"She's far from my type."

"Oh? You seem like you'd go for gorgeous and sophisticated. So then what is your type?"

The way his fabulous blue-gray eyes delved into mine sent my pulse thrumming.

"I'm not sure. Guess I'll know it when I see it." His gaze held mine a moment longer, then he shifted it over to one of the platters and helped himself to another piece of steak.

We finished the rest of the meal chatting about all the things we loved about Louisiana, and it became abundantly clear that Jaxon adored this part of the country and never planned on leaving it.

It wasn't until we were having coffee and dessert that he brought up the subject of the bed-and-breakfast.

"Any idea what you're going to do?" he asked.

I shook my head. "None. I've tried weighing the pros and cons, but they seem to be equally distributed."

He took a sip of coffee, then leaned back in his chair. "I don't know if this'll help with your decision, but I promised Asa I'd stay on and manage the B&B. Of course, only if you want me to," he quickly added.

I tried to hide my shock, but it was clear that I hadn't done a very good job, because his bronzed skin now had a slightly ruddy cast to it.

"I wasn't trying to put you on the spot or anything," he said. "And I'm certainly not begging for a job. Believe me, I won't have the least bit of trouble finding another one if need be."

I didn't want to make him defensive. It's just that he'd really thrown me off guard. "Thank you so much for the offer. And if I do decide to stay here and open a bed-and-breakfast, I'll definitely think seriously about having you run it."

He quickly chugged down the rest of his coffee,

then set the cup in the saucer. "Good enough. I just wanted you to know I'd be here if you needed me. It was important to your grandfather that you not be left on your own." He pushed back his chair and stood. "Good night, Olivia."

After he left, I took a few more bites of dessert, then pushed the plate away. I had no idea what to make of that man. One minute he made me so angry I could scream, and the next he had me thinking he was someone I could come to trust and depend on. Not to mention the fact that he sent my heart racing like it had been charged with jolts of electricity.

As I was about to head up to my room, Theresa arrived and began to clear the table.

"You wouldn't happen to know if there's Wi-Fi here, would you?" I asked.

"Oh, yes, Miss Olivia, there is. I use the Internet all the time."

"Would you be able to get me the password and network key? I'd like to email my friends back home tonight."

"Come with me," she answered.

I followed her into my grandfather's study, where she went over to an old rolltop desk and opened a drawer. She took out a small notebook, flipped through the pages, and then wrote the information on a sticky note next to the phone.

"Here ya go," she said, ripping it off the pad and handing it to me.

"Thank you."

When I was upstairs in my room, I sprawled out on the bed, signed onto the Internet, and sent Kelly an email explaining my dilemma. She immediately wrote back, in her usual blunt style, asking if I was insane for having trouble making a decision. How could I not jump at the chance to own a plantation and become filthy rich? She also wanted to know if I'd contacted Dale.

I got a knot in my stomach every time I thought of him. I might not be madly in love, but I cared deeply. I didn't want to hurt him, and moving to Louisiana, even if only for six months, would do just that.

I snapped my laptop closed. Better to say nothing until I made up my mind. And there was someone I needed to talk to who might be able to help me do that. I reached for my cell phone and dialed home. It only rang twice before I heard my father's familiar baritone voice say hello.

"Hi, Daddy!"

"Livvy Luv! It's so great to hear from you. How are you surviving Turnberry?"

"Okay, I guess. Grandpa looks worse than I thought he would, and he didn't come down for dinner like he'd planned."

"Aw, sweetie. I'm sorry, but that's why he wanted to spend time with you...you know, before..." His voice trailed off, and I knew he couldn't say the words because he was thinking of what happened to Mom.

"That's not the only reason why he asked me here." I heard my dad's deep intake of breath as he waited for me to go on. "Grandpa wants to leave me the plantation, along with almost all the rest of his estate."

"I had an idea you'd be in his will, but not to that extent. My goodness, Livvy, you'll be set for life a million times over. You must be overwhelmed."

"That's putting it mildly. But there's a condition to my inheritance. Remember how Mom always wanted to make Turnberry into a bed-and-breakfast?"

"Of course. I'd thought that was a great idea too, and we would have if things had been different." His voice cracked a little.

I waited a second before I went on. "Well, to honor Mom, Grandpa wants me to do that, but I have to stay here for at least six months, or I'll lose my inheritance. After that time, I can move back to Boston if I want, and keep the money he's leaving me. However, the plantation will be given to the historical society."

"A bed-and-breakfast is a huge undertaking, Liv. Do you know what you're going to do?"

"I thought you could help me with that."

"My, my, Livvy Luv. I couldn't do that. It's your life. Only you can decide what to do with it."

I swallowed hard, trying to manage an answer. "But I can't. That's the problem—I don't know. Part of me thinks, why not? It would be a wild new adventure. And part wants to go home now. There are so many memories of Mom here. And besides, what about you? I can't leave you. You'll be alone."

There was a long pause on the other end of the phone. "Dad, are you still there?"

"Yes... Yes... I am. Look Livvy, you can't live my life. You need to live your own. Follow the path that's right for you."

"But Dad—"

He cut me off. "I've been delaying telling you something. Seems like this is the right time. I met someone. We've gone out a few times—once for coffee and once for dinner. I didn't want to say anything until I knew for sure she might be someone I'd actually want to date on a regular basis."

The shock of what he said hit me full force. "Oh my goodness, Dad. Are you kidding me?"

"This doesn't in any way change my feelings for your mom."

"Dad! Don't be ridiculous. I'm so happy for you. I hated seeing you so miserable. You need someone in your life. Mom's been gone a long time. She'd want you to move on as much as I do."

"Have I told you lately what a special person you are?"

"All the time."

"You'll make the right choice, Liv. You always do. Just follow your heart."

"Thanks, Dad. Love you."

"Back at you."

It wasn't until after I hung up the phone that I realized I had tears running down my cheeks. A large weight had been lifted from my shoulders. My dad might actually find a little happiness. I was so grateful for that. However, I still had to decide what to do.

~ⱺ⳿ⱺ⳿ⱺ⳿~

MOONLIGHT STREAMED IN through the bedroom window, and the cypress trees, draped in Spanish moss just outside it, were cast as shadows on the wall. They looked like monsters moving back and forth as the wind blew their branches around.

I closed my eyes, but sleep eluded me. My mind was awhirl. How was I going to give my grandfather an answer in the morning? I thought of my mom and wondered what she'd want me to do. She used to give the best advice, and I wished more than ever that she was still here. With an overwhelming desire to feel closer to her, I grabbed the terrycloth robe at the end of the bed.

After slipping it on, I headed down the hall, stopping in front of a closed door. My hand shook a little as I turned the knob.

It was pitch-black inside, so I ran my hand over the wall until I found the light switch. The room, now bathed in an eerie golden glow, looked exactly the same as the last time I was there—feminine and beautiful, just like my mom had been. I walked over to the antique four-poster and sat on it. I could visualize her lying there, and I could almost smell her perfume. "What should I do, Mom?" I whispered, holding my head in my hands. I sat there for a long while, oblivious to the time, half expecting to hear her voice. But of course, that didn't happen.

I got up and headed for the door. As I reached for the wall switch to turn off the light, my indecision disappeared. It was as if my mom had found a way to communicate with me. I knew without a doubt that this bed-and-breakfast opportunity had been given to me for a reason, and I needed to pursue it. Not just because that was what my mom would want me to do, but because I'd be saving my family's heritage. My grandfather had faith that I was up for this challenge, and I needed to do it for him and the other Turnberrys before him.

For the first time since arriving here, I felt the weight I'd been carrying dissolve. I didn't want to wait until morning to talk to Grandfather, so I raced down the hall toward his room.

After two knocks on his door, I heard my grandfather grumble what sounded like "Come in." I peeked inside. The lamp on his nightstand was on, and he had a book resting on his chest, as if he might have dozed off while reading.

"I'm sorry if I woke you."

A half smile lit his drawn features. "Come in, my dear. Come in."

As I neared his bed, I realized that beads of perspiration soaked his forehead. "Grandpa, are you all right?"

He scrunched up his face as if in pain before answering. "Just those darn night sweats."

I thought there might be more bothering him than that, but I didn't press the issue.

He glanced at the clock on the table next to him. ""What brings you here at midnight?"

It was evident by the hopeful gleam in his eyes what answer he was looking for, and I was glad that I could provide that to him.

"I want you to know how honored I am that you have so much faith in me that you want to leave Turnberry in my hands. I'll do everything possible to make you and my mom proud."

His pasty complexion brightened a little. "You've made me very happy, Livvy." He looked up at the ceiling. "Did you hear that, Annie? Your daughter is going to fulfill your dream." He tried to sit up more in bed, but was overcome with a hacking cough.

I plumped up his pillows, and when he seemed more comfortable, he said, "Water...Livvy."

I ran from the room. As I headed down the hallway, one of the bedroom doors swung open, and Jaxon stepped out.

"Everything okay?" he asked as I raced by.

"My grandfather just had a terrible coughing fit. I'm going to get him something to drink. Will you please stay with him for a minute?"

"Of course."

I ran down the staircase, through the vestibule, and on toward the kitchen. Once there, I opened a cabinet and took out a glass. On the shelf above it, I spotted a pitcher. As I reached for it, a plastic bag with what looked like sugar inside dropped out onto the counter. I shoved it back onto the shelf and then filled the pitcher with water, adding a few ice cubes, and then headed back upstairs.

Jaxon was standing next to my grandfather's

bed, talking to him in a hushed tone.

"Here you go, Grandpa," I said, pouring him a glass of water and holding it for him as he took a sip, then I set the glass and pitcher on the bedside table. He looked paler than before, and my chest tightened with worry. "Maybe I should call the doctor."

He shook his head. "I just need some sleep. There's nothing the doctor can do anyway. Besides, you've made me so happy, Livvy. I'll sleep peacefully now that you've accepted my proposition. And Jaxon was telling me he offered his services to you. You should take him up on it. He's a good man. One of the best I've ever known. He'll make sure this place is run with precision. And who knows, maybe someday the two of you can put that ridiculous feud between our families to rest."

I felt my cheeks grow hot as I glanced over at Jaxon.

"Asa, you know that anything I can do for you, I will, and that goes for your granddaughter too. Within reason, of course..." he said, referring to Asa's attempt at matchmaking.

I leaned over and kissed my grandfather's

cheek. "Good night. I'll see you in the morning."

He smiled and then closed his eyes. "Good night, Olivia."

Jaxon and I left the bedroom, and for the first time since running into him in the hall, I realized I was wearing night clothes. I pulled my robe closed tighter, hiding my thin cotton gown. He still had on the clothes he'd worn at dinner. Only his shirt was open more, exposing his broad, muscular chest. I shifted my gaze, not wanting to stare. But it was too late. His firm mouth curled, leaving no doubt that he knew he was a very attractive man. One who few women could resist.

"For what it's worth," he said, "I wish you much success with the bed-and-breakfast, whether I stay on at Turnberry or not. Who knows, you may prove me wrong and turn out to be a country girl at heart." Despite his words, there was a gleam in his eyes and a crisp tone in his voice that held a challenge.

"I can't promise that I'll stay here forever, but I assure you it'll be at least six months. Good night, Jaxon." Without waiting for a response, I walked away, leaving him standing in the hall.

When I was back in my room and settled in

bed, I pulled the covers up over my head, as if that would block out the image of his handsome face. There was something about him that was so familiar, that, crazy as it might sound, I felt like I knew exactly what it would feel like to be held in his arms. Yet at the same time, he irritated me like no man I'd ever known. How could someone that I barely knew extract such strong feelings from me? I thought of Dale back in Boston, patiently awaiting my return. He'd never evoked emotions like that from me. Maybe that was the problem. I closed my eyes, and as I drifted off to sleep, I knew I needed to tell him in the morning that I wouldn't be coming back...at least not for quite a while.

Chapter Five

I WOKE TO the sound of banging on the door and the loud whine of sirens. I shot up in bed and grabbed my robe. My heart was thundering as I raced for the door. Something must've happened to my grandfather.

Uncle Paul stood in the hall, his face sallow and drawn. "Liv, Asa's gone."

My hands flew up to my mouth, and I thought my chest was going to explode. "Oh no! I was just with him a few hours ago. I went to his room around midnight to tell him I would open the bed-and-breakfast. I never thought that..." My voice broke and my throat tightened up. There was no way I could say those words. Instead, tears streamed down my cheeks. "W-what needs to be done?"

"The paramedics are with him now, and Dr. Becker is on his way. He'll make the declaration, and then the body can be picked up by the mortuary." His voice was cold and matter-of-fact, and I attributed that to shock.

"I want to see him. I need to see him." Without waiting for an answer, I rushed past him down the hall to my grandfather's bedroom.

Standing outside the door was Jess, her face red and blotchy. Next to her was Jaxon, and behind him Theresa and a few other staff. I peered inside the room to see a bevy of paramedics around his bed, so that I couldn't get a look at my grandfather. Just as I was about to step inside, loud footsteps thundered down the hall. A moment later, a small, thin man carrying a black medical bag pushed inside. He was with Asa for a few minutes before joining us out in the hall.

"I'm so very sorry for your loss," Dr. Becker said to us all before shifting his gaze over to Jaxon. "You're using Kaylene Funeral Home?"

Jaxon nodded.

"I'll give them a call now." He pulled a cell phone from his pocket.

Before he dialed the number, I asked, "Is it all right if I spend a moment with him?"

The doctor's eyes were full of compassion. "Of course. Take all the time you need."

I waited for the paramedics to pack their bags and leave before going over to the bed. At first it looked like my grandfather was just sleeping, but then I saw the blue tinge to his lips and skin, making this all too real. "Grandpa, why did you have to leave so soon? I barely got to spend any time with you. I'm so sorry that I didn't get to visit after Mom died. It was just too painful for Dad to come back...and for me too. I'm so grateful for yesterday, though, and for coming to see you earlier. It would've broken my heart if you'd left before I had a chance to give you my decision. I'll take care of Turnberry. I promise. I'll make it the best bed-and-breakfast in Louisiana." Tears streamed down my cheeks and into my mouth, and my throat burned. "Mom has you now, and I'm happy that she's no longer alone." I took hold of his cold hand and squeezed it. "Good-bye. I love you."

When I left his room, my heart and mind were numb. My legs felt like rubber as I walked, not knowing or caring where I was headed. A fog came over me, and I felt like I was falling until a strong arm around my waist put me back on my feet.

"Good thing I was close enough to catch you," Jaxon said, staring down at me.

"Catch me?"

"You almost took a nosedive."

"Really? I'm sorry. This all just seems so unreal, and it brings back memories that I'd rather not have."

"You don't need to explain."

I looked up into his blue-gray eyes. "Does this make me a weak city girl?"

"A city girl? Yes. Weak? No. You have every right to be light-headed."

"Thanks." I offered him a slight smile.

"You'll feel better after having breakfast."

I made a face. "I can't even think of food."

"How about something to drink?"

I ran my tongue over my dry, parched lips. "That I can handle. But first I need to get dressed," I said, looking down at my bathrobe.

"Probably a good idea. I'll meet you in the parlor in twenty minutes."

"Okay." After I left him, I took a shower and picked out what to wear, all while in a daze. It wasn't until I was downstairs and seated in an old overstuffed chair that I realized my pants and shirt didn't match. Not that I cared what I had on, but my fashion faux pas seemed even more apparent when Jess walked into the parlor looking as beautiful and perfect as ever. She set down the tray that she was carrying and handed me a glass of sweet tea.

Thankful for the cool beverage, I took a long drink. A moment later, Jaxon came in with a basket of blueberry muffins.

"Dottie just baked these. They're still warm. Try one." He held the basket out in front of me.

"I don't think I could get it down."

"Try just a little."

It was obvious he wasn't going to give up until I took one, so I reached inside and pulled out a muffin. "Thanks." I couldn't manage more than a couple of bites. After that, I felt like I was going to choke, so I set it down on a napkin on the side table next to me.

Jessica was picking at hers as well. "My dad said you've decided to stay here and do the bed-and-breakfast thing?" Her words were cool and tinged with jealousy.

I felt bad for her. It wasn't her fault her father was a gambler. Yet, Grandfather barely left her anything because of that. "I think it's the right thing to do. At least give it my best shot." I shifted my gaze over to Jaxon, who was seated across the room from us. "And Jax is going to stay on and help run it."

His eyes locked with mine as he smiled his approval, but when I looked back at Jess, it was impossible to read her emotions. However, something flicked across her face that I couldn't decipher, giving me the impression there was more to their relationship than I was aware of. I knew that was ridiculous. Jaxon had told me so, and I had no reason to disbelieve him. My cousin's emotions were probably just running helter-skelter this morning, the same as mine were. "You know, Jess, I could use your help too. If you'd like to stay here awhile and help me redecorate some of the rooms, that would be wonderful." I don't know why I said that. The thought just popped into my head, and it seemed to be a charitable thing to offer.

Her face lit up. "I'd love to help. I'm really good at decorating."

"Great. That's settled, then. I feel so much

better knowing you'll both be here."

The mood in the room seemed to lighten some, and we chatted awhile, throwing out ideas for paint colors and new furniture. When I took the last sip of tea, my stomach cramped and I thought I might get sick. Maybe it was because it was extra sweet at the bottom or just because my grandfather's passing had caught up with me, but I excused myself and went up to my room.

I barely made it to the bathroom before my stomach revolted. I don't know how long I was in there. It seemed like hours. But finally, I began to feel a little better. After brushing my teeth and washing my face, I climbed into bed and fell asleep. When I woke, I was in the dark, and I realized I'd slept the entire day. I tried to sit up, but the room spun, so I lay back down and fell asleep again.

The next time I woke, it was morning, and I was feeling much better. Before I started my day, I needed to let my loved ones in Boston know what had happened to my grandfather. Kelly would be the easiest, since her favorite way to communicate was through email. She wasn't a phone person.

I reached over to the side table next to the bed for my laptop. But when I turned it on, it requested the network information that I'd put in the other day. I hadn't thought I'd need it again, so I'd thrown away the paper Theresa had written it on.

I quickly put on some clothes and headed down to my grandfather's study, and then over to his old rolltop desk. I opened the drawer and pulled out what I thought would be the notebook Theresa had gotten the network key from, but instead I held a leather-bound journal. I flipped through the pages and realized it was my grandfather's diary. I snapped it closed, feeling like it would be wrong to read his innermost thoughts. Maybe someday. After all, it would surely help me to come to know him better. But not now. Not so soon after his death.

I stuck the journal back in the drawer and slid my hand over to the side of it, where I located the notebook I'd been looking for. After copying down the network key, I put the notebook back in the drawer and headed upstairs to my room.

Telling Kelly about my grandfather's death was far easier than telling either my dad or Dale. Although my dad wasn't surprised by the news, I could tell it upset him greatly nonetheless. And Dale was difficult because I also had to break the news that I was staying in Louisiana a lot longer than planned. He was nice and polite as always and still willing to wait for me, despite my telling him not to. I should have pressed the issue, but I didn't have the energy to do so right now.

My stomach gurgled, and for the first time in over a day, I realized I was hungry. As I was about to enter the kitchen, I overheard two of the staff discussing my grandfather's death.

"Theresa said when she was bringin' Mr. Turnberry some soup, she saw a dark ghostly figure standin' over his bed, and then the next mornin', he was dead."

"It was seen before Miss Ann died too, and then soon after dat when Cammy took sick, and she wasn't even a Turnberry."

"Accordin' to the curse, anyone at the plantation can fall victim to it and die."

I was too stunned to say anything. When I was a kid, I'd heard rumors of a curse that had been put on the house back in the 1800s by Tucker Sheldon, manager of the Clairmont Plantation. My dad had dispelled such talk as nonsense, not wanting me to be frightened. Apparently, though, the rumor still existed and the staff believed in such things.

I cleared my throat to let them know that I

stood there and then walked inside. "Am I too late for breakfast?"

A short, stout woman shook her head. "I've got some sweet potato pancakes here dat should still be hot." She reached over to a warming oven and pulled out a plate.

"Sounds wonderful."

Her eyes grew wide when I sat on one of the stools at the counter. "Miss Olivia, I can fix this up for ya and bring it to the dinin' room. Ya'll be much more comfortable in there."

"There's no need to be so formal today. Besides, it's no fun to eat alone." The two women shrugged and went about their routines while I ate. "I heard you talking about a ghost and a curse," I said between bites.

"I'm so sorry, Miss Olivia. We meant no disrespect," the stout woman said.

"It's okay. It's not like I'd never heard of it before."

"But yar grandfather didn't like it when we spoke of it."

"It doesn't bother me. I don't believe in such things. I was wondering about the woman you mentioned, though. Cammy. She was a cook here, right?"

"Yeah, not for long, though. Less than six months. Right, Molly?"

The other woman nodded. "She started shortly before yar mom...died. Worked at Clairmont before dat."

"Hmm, I didn't know that. You'd said she'd gotten sick. Do you know what she died from?"

"No, just dat she'd gotten ill suddenly."

"Just like my mom," I said under my breath.

"I know ya don't believe in such things, Miss Olivia, but ya should know dat's how the curse works. One day ya're fine, and then the next, sick as a dog. Ya might even think ya're gettin' better, but ya're not. Once it takes hold, there's no gettin' rid of it."

Despite knowing better, I couldn't help but think of what had happened to me yesterday and how sick I'd been. However, common sense quickly took over, and I knew that had nothing to do with a silly curse.

I needed to put all these superstitions to rest, and that meant coming to terms with the past too. I needed to clean out my mother's bedroom.

~e෮෮෮~

It was a dark and dreary day. Not rainy, just cloudy and dank. And that didn't help the atmosphere in my mom's room.

I set down on the floor the big box I was carrying and went over to the window, opening it wide to let in some much-needed fresh air.

Outside, I spotted Jaxon talking to a gardener. He must've heard the window open, because he looked up and waved at me. I waved back, glad I'd decided to take him up on the offer to help with the running of the bed-and-breakfast. Without him, I would've been lost.

I stood there a few moments longer before getting to work packing up my mom's things. I'd just about filled the box when something scurried past my foot.

A small black mouse ran across the room and into the closet. Great. I sure didn't need a rodent problem. When I went over to the closet, the mouse scooted up against the back wall and then disappeared into what had to be a hole in the floorboard. I got down on my knees and ran my hand along the floor. Not only did I find a hole but there was a crack that went up the side of the wall about four feet, over about three, and then back down to the floor. The door was nearly invisible. I pushed on it, but nothing happened. I pushed again, this time harder, and it opened, revealing a small, dark room.

I had to stoop down to get inside, and before I realized what was happening, the door swung shut. I opened my mouth to scream, but nothing came out. Suddenly, I felt like I was falling off the side of a mountain, and the speed that I was going down sucked my breath away. When I hit the ground, the world went black.

Chapter Six

Turnberry House Plantation – Louisiana, 1831

"JANE, WAKE UP!" A small, soft voice cried.

My head ached, and someone was shaking my shoulders.

"Ya must've fainted," the same woman proclaimed.

I opened my eyes, but everything spun, so I squeezed them shut.

"Jane, please get up. We have to get out of here."

Jane? I opened my eyes again and realized I was in a cramped, dark place. I was half sitting and half lying down, with my legs draped over someone's thighs.

"Who are you and why do you keep calling me Jane?" I asked, rubbing my head as I sat up fully.

"Oh, dear. Ya must've hit yar head harder than it appeared." Her voice was tinged with concern.

"Don't worry. She'll be fine. Give her a few minutes, and I'm sure her memory'll return." This time, a man spoke.

"Where am I, and who are you people?"

The woman sighed. "I'm Mary, he's Nathan, and we're in a heap of trouble. If we don't get out of here now, we might not have another chance."

"Another chance at what?" I was totally confused. Images were popping in and out of my head, and faces of people I loved, like my dad and Kelly, were fading. The harder I tried to keep them there, the more difficult it became.

"Another chance to escape," Nathan said, slipping his arms under mine and hoisting me onto my feet.

I wavered a little, but both of them now had a hold of me.

Nathan opened the door a crack and then all the way. A woman stood outside the closet and waved for us to come out. She had curly blonde hair and wore the most beautiful gown I'd ever seen. She looked vaguely familiar to me, but I didn't know how or why.

"Hurry," she said softly. "There's a wagon waitin' round back, by the sugar house."

She led the way, and we followed her down the rear stairs and into the pantry, then out the kitchen door. "Don't worry," she said, sensing our concern, "no one's around. They're all at chapel. But our time's runnin' out."

We raced through the gardens and out a white swinging gate, past rows of slave quarters and a number of other buildings until we reached the sugar house. Sure enough, in front of it was a wagon full of bundles of freshly milled raw sugar.

"See there," she said, pointing to the front of the wagon, "the boards dip down enough for you to hide if you lie flat. Then Bentley will cover you with sugar and take you to a safe house."

The wagon's driver tipped his hat at us. Nathan wasted no time helping Mary in, but when he reached for me, the blonde woman grabbed his arm.

"There's only room for two," she announced.

His jaw dropped, and his brow furrowed. "Then I stay."

Mary gasped. "Nathan, no. Tucker'll kill ya."

"She's right," the woman added. "For all we know, he might already have the hounds out. This is your only chance to leave. You and Mary deserve to get married and live a good life. That'll never happen here." She looked over at me. "And don't worry about Jane. There's a hollowed-out area along the riverbank where she can hide until a boat comes for her. Ellis has it all taken care of."

As if on cue, a man walked toward us. He was tall and handsome, with muscles rippling under his elegant white shirt. He had golden hair that hung down across his forehead, nearly covering one gorgeous brown eye. He reached his hand out to me and when I took it, my heart thundered. I knew Ellis Clairmont well. Memories of this strange time and place came flooding back, and those of my dad and Kelly disappeared.

"Go on, Nathan. Time's a wastin'. Don't worry. I won't let anythin' happen to Jane." His grip on my hand tightened, and I knew he meant what he said.

We watched the wagon disappear out of view, then the blonde woman, who I now recognized as my half sister, Sarah, hugged me tight, tears spilling from her eyes.

"I'm goin' to miss you so much. Stay safe, dear one," she cried.

I kissed her cheek, fighting back my own tears. "Watch over my ma," I said before Ellis led me away.

When we reached the base of a giant cypress tree dripping with Spanish moss, he stopped and took me in his arms. His mouth sought mine. His kiss was gentle at first, but then it turned more demanding. His tongue sent shivers of desire racing through me, and for a moment, I almost forgot the gravity of my situation.

When our lips parted, grief and despair tore at my heart. "How could you do this to me?" I cried.

"Shhh, keep your voice down."

"I don't care who hears me. I don't care about anythin' now."

"Don't say that. If anythin' were to happen to you, I don't know what I'd do."

I looked up at him with anger and disbelief. "What do you think your fiancée would say if she knew you'd promised yourself to me?"

"You know about my upcomin' marriage to Sarah?"

"How could you have thought I wouldn't find

out? And to think I'd been so stupid as to trust you. I believed every word you told me. But you lied. How can I trust you now? How do I know you're not leadin' me right into a trap and to my death?"

"Jane, how could you say that? I never lied about my feelin's for you...about my love."

"Yet you're goin' to marry Sarah. Is it because she's a Turnberry—a legitimate one who can produce an heir that would tie the two largest plantations in the region together forever? Is that why?"

"If there was any way out of this nightmare, I would take it. I went to my father, you know. I told him I didn't love Sarah and couldn't marry her. He laughed and said I was a hopeless romantic, and if I didn't marry her, he'd have Lewis do so in my place. And do you know what that would mean? Sarah and I wouldn't be able to help any more of your people. They'd stay slaves and be beaten and abused even worse than Nathan had been. My little brother is as brutal as Tucker, and together, they'd terrorize both Clairmont and Turnberry. What do you think would happen to Ellen? Your dad wouldn't be able to protect her against the likes of those two."

I knew he was right about everything he said. My ma would be in terrible danger. Ellis had no choice but to marry Sarah.

"Your boat should be here soon. But you've got to stay out of sight until then. You can hide down here." He took my hand and started to walk over to the hollowed-out section of the riverbank that Sarah had mentioned.

However, footsteps behind us made us stop, and when we spun around, we were face-to-face with Tucker Sheldon. His beady black eyes glittered dangerously, reminding me of a rattlesnake about to strike.

"Did you think I wasn't aware of your little midnight rendezvous?" His laugh had an evil cackle to it. "Nothin' gets by me...not that, and not the fact that you helped those two no good slaves escape, and you're goin' to pay for that regardless of who you are—Clairmont heir or not."

Cold, hard steel whisked by in a flash, the tip of the knife landing in Ellis's shoulder. Tucker pulled it out, sending blood spraying over us, but when he went to strike again, this time Ellis was ready for him. He pushed me out of the way and was able to dodge the blade. However, Ellis was no match for a madman with a knife. Tucker stabbed at him again, this time making contact just inches away from the first wound.

I had to do something before he killed Ellis. I glanced around and saw an oak branch a few feet away. It must've come down during the last storm. I picked it up and with all my might whacked Tucker over the back of his head. He went down hard.

I raced over to Ellis, then ripped off the bottom of my skirt, using the cloth to stop the bleeding by wrapping it around his shoulder and tying the ends tightly. "You need to have this tended to." My bottom lip quivered as I viewed the amount of blood soaking his shirt.

"Don't worry about me. I'll be fine. It's you—" His words were cut off sharply when Tucker staggered to his feet and then lunged at Ellis. The two men exchanged blows at the edge of the riverbank. The fight ended abruptly when Tucker fell into the water and a strong current swept him under.

He came up long enough to shout out a curse. "You'll pay for this, and all the Turnberrys to come. I'll be back to get my revenge. No one on the plantation will be immune. Count on it!" And then the water pulled him down and he was gone.

I covered my face with my hands.

Ellis gently moved them to my sides and stared directly into my eyes. "I'll love you forever, Jane. Nothin' will ever change that." His last words were smothered on my lips. His vow sealed with a kiss was both delicious and heartbreaking.

Off in the distance, the sound of dogs barking pierced the silence. "You have to go now, Jane."

I opened my mouth, but no words came out.

"Run, as fast as you can. Stay close to the water's edge. When you spot a boat with a red stripe on its side, wave your arms. They'll pick you up.

As I started to run, Ellis said, "We'll be together again, someday...somewhere. I promise."

I'd gone about ten yards when I felt my spinel necklace drop. I put my hands up to my neck, trying to grab it, but it was gone. There was no time to stop and look for it. The dogs were fast approaching. I glanced over my shoulder as I ran and saw that Ellis had found it. That was the last image I had of him.

I ran and ran until I didn't think I could run any longer. Dusk had set in, and there was no boat in sight. I had to keep going, though, no matter how tired I was. My eyes were blurred by exhaustion, so I didn't see the log in front of me until it was too late. I fell hard and hit my head on the ground, and then everything went black.

Chapter Seven

Present Day – Louisiana

WHEN I WOKE, I was in the dark. The last thing I remembered was being out of breath from running. I slid my hands over the walls, realizing I was in the secret room behind the closet, but I had no idea how I'd gotten there.

I opened the door a crack. Standing in the middle of the bedroom was a strikingly handsome, tawny-haired man holding my spinel pendant.

I put my hands up to my neck, and sure enough, my necklace was gone. I squinted, trying to bring everything into better focus. Images of Ellis, Mary, Nathan, and that horrible Tucker Sheldon faded in and out, and then something warm and furry ran over my legs. Without thinking, I screamed. A second later, the door was pushed open wide, the mouse scampered out, and in front of me stood that gorgeous man.

"Livvy, what are you doing?" He stuck his head in the room and looked around.

As I stared into his fabulous blue-gray eyes, memories came rushing back. I remembered packing up my mom's things and then finding this little hideaway. My necklace must've fallen off in the middle of it all.

I stepped into the bedroom, and he followed. "I must've passed out from the heat in there," I said, wiping my forehead with the back of my hand. "And then I had the most unbelievable dream. It was back in the 1800s, and I was there with my great-great-great aunt Sarah Turnberry. Only in the dream, I was her half sister, a light-skinned Creole slave named Jane. And the necklace you're holding, it fell off my neck as I was running away, hoping to gain freedom. Ellis Clairmont found it." My voice cracked when I said his name. "It's been passed down from generation to generation since then. My mom gave it to me when I was a little girl."

"And Ellis gave it to William Turnberry for

safekeeping," Jaxon added, looking down at the spinel pendant in his hands.

My mouth dropped open. "He did?"

"According to his journal."

"You have it?"

I was surprised at how his eyes sparkled with excitement. "Yes, and it recounts everything that you just told me, and then some."

My bottom lip trembled. "How is it possible that a dream would mimic history?"

He shrugged. "Maybe it wasn't a dream."

I took a deep sharp breath. "Well, what else could it have been?"

"Maybe you were experiencing a past life."

I stared at him in astonishment. "Nonsense. Don't tell me you believe in such things."

There were touches of humor around his mouth and eyes. "This is Louisiana, remember, the heart of Cajun country. We're a superstitious lot."

I knew that to be true. My mom had been. "Would you mind if I have a look at the journal sometime?"

He shook his head decisively. "Of course not. Our families have been tied together by generations, even if they did have a falling-out over a century ago."

Jaxon checked the clasp on the spinel necklace before placing it around my neck. "You need to be sure it closes tightly when you put it on," he advised. Tingles ran up my back at the touch of his fingers on my skin—so familiar, so welcome that I closed my eyes, savoring every moment of it. When I opened them, he was staring at me with an odd expression on his face. My cheeks burned with embarrassment for having reacted so strangely to his touch.

"Thank you," I said, readjusting the pendant and then moving away from him by crossing the room and picking up the box I'd filled with my mom's things.

A second later, he was at my side and reaching out to me. "I'll get that."

I handed him the box, being careful not to let our fingers touch.

"Where do you want it?"

"I thought I'd donate it to charity."

"The church rummage sale is in a few weeks. I can drop it off there, if you'd like."

"That's perfect. Thanks."

"No problem."

I followed him downstairs, and after he put the box in the trunk of his car, we went over the plans he'd been discussing earlier with the gardener. Jaxon thought it would be a good idea to remove some of the overgrown shrubbery that contained thorns, since we'd be giving tours of the garden to our guests. I had to agree that the possibility that someone might get pricked was high, so those bushes had to go.

He was full of lots of wonderful ideas, like redoing all the plantation buildings to their original design, making them historically accurate, including the slave quarters. As he spoke, once again I had the feeling that I knew him much better than I actually did.

The next two days went by in a whirl as I spent them dealing with painters and carpenters, leaving little time for me to dwell on my grandfather's death.

I left his funeral arrangements up to Uncle Paul and Jessica, since I wasn't familiar with Southern traditions. It wasn't until I was getting dressed for it that it really sank in that he was gone. As I zipped up my black dress, I fought back tears and wished my dad were here. Although he offered to come to support me, I knew it would be difficult for him to get away, and it wasn't as if Grandfather and he had been overly close. After all, he'd taken my mom away from Turnberry to move to Boston. It was clear every time we came to visit that Asa had never fully forgiven him for that, despite the fact that my mom had promised to come back one day and turn this place into a bed-and-breakfast.

I pulled my hair up into a twist and then checked my appearance in the mirror. For the first time, I could honestly say I did look very much like my mother, and that thought brought me great comfort and would provide me the strength needed to get through the day.

~◦⋐◦⋑◦~

IT SEEMED LIKE the entire town of Kaylene had come out to attend my grandfather's simple gravesite service. The long procession walked through my family's private cemetery, following a trio of jazz musicians playing brass band tunes. At the site, people lined up around the coffin, which was covered with a fringed black cloth.

When the service was over, I stayed behind to visit my mom's grave, while everyone else went up to the house for something to eat. The kitchen staff had spent days preparing casseroles of every possible variety, several bean dishes, and numerous platters of devilled eggs.

As I stood in front of her gravestone, the clouds parted and the gray sky that had plagued us for the past few days was replaced with a robin's egg blue. I took that as a sign that she was pleased that I'd come to visit. "I think you'd be proud of me, Mom. The bed-and-breakfast is coming along better than I ever thought possible. Of course, it's not all my doing. Jessica has been a big help, and Jaxon Carter, Jonathon Clairmont's nephew, is going to be helping me run it. I couldn't have done any of this without him."

"That's not true."

I spun around at the sound of Jaxon's voice. His tall, black-clad figure projected power and strength. His massive shoulders filled his jacket, and his stance emphasized his thighs and the slimness of his hips.

"I'm confident you would've done just fine without me, and I know your mom is very proud of you," he remarked.

"Thanks for saying that."

"You don't have to thank me for stating the truth." He reached into his jacket pocket and pulled out a journal. "Here." He handed it to me. "You'd mentioned that you wanted to read about Ellis's life. I wanted to give this to you before I forgot."

My fingers tingled as I ran them over the worn leather, and I felt a oneness with the man who'd written his deepest thoughts inside.

I'll leave you alone now," Jaxon added. "I didn't mean to interrupt."

I stuffed the journal into my handbag and then grabbed his arm. "You're not interrupting. I was just about to go back to the house. I'll walk there with you."

When we reached the French parterre garden, I stopped at the fountain, watching the angel spew water. "I can't stop thinking about what happened in that secret room I found inside my mom's closet. I'm not saying I believe in past lives or anything like that, but if I did, how would I know for sure whether what I experienced the other day with Ellis and Sarah and Jane was that or just a regular old dream?"

He studied me closely, a faint smile curving the corners of his mouth. "*If* you believed in such things, I'd say you should meet with someone experienced in past life regression."

"Past life regression? And how would I find someone like that?"

"I'm sure New Orleans has plenty. I could get you a name, if you'd like."

"You wouldn't mind?"

"Not at all. I have to say, I'm quite curious myself at what happened to you." His voice was deep and husky.

We walked through the rest of the garden in silence until we reached the back patio. It was filled with people and the sounds of trumpets, trombones, and tubas. The musicians who'd led the procession had set up out there. My grandfather's funeral was more like a bon voyage party than a time to mourn, and I had the feeling he would have approved of that.

"I'd like you to meet my mother and stepfather," Jaxon said, heading over to a handsome middle-aged couple leaning up against the patio wall.

The woman had the same tawny hair and blue-gray eyes as Jaxon. She held out a slim hand. "I'm Cynthia. It's so nice to meet you."

"And I'm Nigel." His handshake was firm and confident, matching his distinguished demeanor. Tall—though not as tall as Jax—and sinewy, with streaks of silver hair at both temples, he reminded me of a college professor.

"It's a pleasure to meet you both." I wondered if Jonathon Clairmont was here too.

As if reading my mind, Cynthia said, "I'm sorry my brother couldn't make it to Asa's funeral. Jon is away on business, but he asked me to offer you his condolences."

"Thank you. I appreciate that."

"How are you liking our fine state so far?" Nigel asked with a cool, appraising look.

Before I could answer, Jessica rushed up to me and sputtered, "I'm sorry to interrupt, but you're needed in the kitchen right away."

"Excuse me." I had to run to keep up with my cousin, and when I reached the doorway to the kitchen, the two workers who'd made me sweet potato pancakes the other day were huddled on the floor together crying.

I knelt beside them. "What's wrong?"

The short, stout woman answered. "Molly saw that awful ghost of Tucker Sheldon." The woman's mouth trembled as she hugged her friend.

"Miss Olivia, that means I'm goin' to die," Molly wailed.

I took her chin in my hand and tilted it up so she looked directly into my eyes. "You are not going to die," I said firmly.

"But I know what I saw." She sniffled.

"Where did this happen?"

"The back hall. I was goin' upstairs with a plate of food for yar Uncle Paul. He was in his room. Said he needed some quiet. Dat's when I saw dat horrible black shadow."

"Maybe that's all it was...just a shadow."

Molly looked at me like I was dense.

"I know the difference between a ghost and a regular old shadow." She started to sob uncontrollably again.

I didn't want to upset her more by downplaying her belief in ghosts. "Molly, try to calm down. You're not going to die. I promise. Take the rest of the day off and go relax." I looked over at the woman beside her. "I'm sorry. I don't know your name."

"I'm Pat," the stout woman replied.

"Why don't you take the day off too and spend it with Molly?"

Pat nodded.

A crowd had formed in the doorway behind Jess. What I didn't need were people spreading rumors of a ghost at Turnberry before I'd even opened the bed-and-breakfast.

Jess must've been worried about the impact of Molly's words too, because she poured her a glass of sweet tea. "This always makes me feel better." She handed the beverage to Molly and then ushered both women out of the kitchen.

After that, the crowd soon dispersed, and I noticed Jaxon resting his shoulder against the doorway, his arms crossed over his chest.

"I told you we're a superstitious lot." His mouth formed into a crooked smile. "You hungry?" He opened the refrigerator, took out a chicken salad casserole, and popped it in the toaster oven.

A few minutes later, we were sitting at the counter on stools, eating the casserole right out of the glass baking dish.

"Your mom and stepdad seem nice," I said, taking a forkful of food.

"My mom's wonderful. Nigel, well, let's just say I've learned to tolerate him. He can be pretty overbearing at times, and for a kid, that can be tough to deal with. As an adult, I take him with a grain of salt." He seemed pensive, not angry.

I regarded him with somber curiosity, wanting to understand him better. "If you don't mind my asking, what happened to your dad?"

He hesitated a minute before answering. "He left when I was twelve. Went back to LA. Life here was too tough for him."

There was no denying the bitterness in his tone, and I knew that was where the comment had come from that he'd made to Jessica about me being a city girl who wouldn't be able to handle life here. I reflected on his pain. There was nothing worse for a young boy than to have his father leave him.

"I could use some fresh air. What about you?" I pushed my stool back and stood.

"Sounds good," he replied, his voice having lost that hardened edge.

Outside, the musicians were packing up and most of the people had left. Just a few stragglers were sitting at a table, polishing off a bottle of whiskey.

We wandered across the lawn, bypassing the gardens as we headed toward the riverbank while serenaded by the cicada's high-pitched song. At the base of an enormous cypress tree covered in Spanish moss, Jaxon stopped walking. I immediately recognized this spot as the one where Jane had said good-bye to Ellis.

"Quite a day, huh?" he asked. "You must be exhausted."

I don't know if everything finally caught up with me, or what, but I was suddenly overcome with emotion. My eyes filled with tears, and before I knew what was happening, I was in Jaxon's arms.

"It's okay to be sad," he whispered against my hair.

"I wish I could've had more time with my grandfather."

"No amount of time is enough. It's always hard to say good-bye to a loved one."

There was such a wistful tone in his voice that I wondered to whom he was referring. And then his mouth covered mine, passionate and demanding, as if this kiss could somehow quell the ache I sensed went through to his soul. I could tell that when he loved, it was deeply, and that his heart had been broken.

Shivers of desire raced through me, something I never experienced with Dale, and I returned Jaxon's kiss with reckless abandon. Standing on tiptoe, I wrapped my arms around his neck, surrendering to my growing passion for this man. What seemed like hours later, we walked back to the house hand in hand.

Sitting out on the patio was Jaxon's mom, stepdad, and Jessica. A slight frown marred her beautiful face as her gaze lingered on us, and once again I couldn't help but wonder if there was something going on between her and Jax. My stomach twisted into a knot. I hoped he wasn't playing me for a fool and leading me down a path of heartbreak.

Chapter Eight

I HADN'T REALIZED how exhausted I was until my head hit the pillow. It wasn't so much sleepy tired as emotionally drained. I thought of the kiss I'd shared with Jaxon and how the touch of his lips had sent a shock wave through my entire body. I'd never felt that before...not ever.

I always knew I'd find the one man who was right for me, and after that intimate moment with Jaxon, my heart was saying I'd found him. It was my head that was holding me back. What if Jax didn't feel the same way about me? What if he really was involved with Jessica somehow? Until I had those questions answered, I wasn't ready to admit that he was the one.

I thought of that fiery bond between Jane and

Ellis. That was what I wanted and needed. Without it, I would never commit myself to anyone.

With a sigh, I reached for my handbag—I'd put it on the nightstand before getting into bed—and took out the small leather-bound journal Jaxon had given me. I flipped through it, stopping to read various passages, and when I came to the part that recounted what I'd experienced in the secret room, all of Jane's hopes and dreams flooded through me.

As I read on, I discovered that Ellis had never gotten over her. Sarah died from some unknown illness about a month after Jane left. However, it was widely blamed on Tucker Sheldon's curse, and that was what started the ill will between the two families. A few years later, Ellis wound up marrying a woman named Catherine Millicent, but she never had his heart.

The following pages were all about business, and his writing became dull and passionless. He'd taken over the running of the plantation after Samuel died.

My eyelids were growing heavier by the second, and the last thing I read before falling asleep was that Ellis was getting ready to go up north on business.

⁓⌾⌾⌾⌾⌾⁓

THE NEXT MORNING, as I was about to go downstairs, I met Uncle Paul in the hallway. He had his suitcase in hand.

"It's time for me head home, Liv. I've been here much longer than planned. Jess says she's staying to help you with the bed-and-breakfast." He kissed my cheek. "I'll see you soon."

After he left, I went to the kitchen, and the first thing I noticed was how quiet the help was. The second was that Molly wasn't there.

Theresa was at the stove, grilling sausage and eggs. Dottie had taken a loaf of cornbread out of a baking pan and was cutting it into squares. And Pat was stirring a pitcher of orange juice. Not only weren't they speaking, but they all wore long faces.

"Good morning," I said, trying to lighten the mood.

"Mornin'," Theresa replied dourly.

"Where's Molly?" My gut told me this glum atmosphere was about her.

Sure enough, Dottie confirmed that by saying,

"She's not been out of her room since yesterday. Been sick as a dog."

"Has anyone called a doctor?" I asked, alarm bells going off in my head.

Pat stared at me. "What good would dat do? Once the curse takes hold, no medicine can cure it."

"That's ridiculous," I said in a tense, clipped voice. Three pairs of eyes were glued to my face.

Theresa put an egg and two sausage links on a plate and handed it to me.

"Would you mind keeping it warm?" I handed it back to her. "I'm going to go see Molly."

"Of course, Miss Olivia." She set the plate on the stove. "If ya go up the back stairs, hers is the third room on the right."

"Thank you."

As I went up the dark, narrow stairway, a sense of uneasiness came over me, so I hurried down the hall, stopping in front of a well-worn wooden door. This was the same oppressive atmosphere that I'd felt in the slave quarters last week.

I knocked on the door a few times before opening it, then I peered inside the small, gloomy room. Molly lay unmoving on the twin bed, a plastic basin beside her. Her face was chalk white, and a line of perspiration glistened above her upper lip.

I walked over to her and touched her hand. "Molly," I said softly.

Her eyes fluttered open, and there were dark purple shadows beneath them. "I'm sorry I didn't make it to work today, Miss Olivia."

"My goodness, I'd never expect you to work when you're ill. Please, don't worry about that. All I want is for you to get better."

Frown lines wrinkled her forehead. "The curse won't let me."

I sat on the edge of the bed and took her cold, clammy hand in mine. "I know you believe the curse is responsible for this, but I happen to think differently. Just the other day, I was as sick as you, but look at me now. I'm fine. No curse. Probably just some food that didn't agree with me."

Her face brightened a bit, but then her frown returned. "I'll bet dat's because ya didn't see Tucker's ghost, did ya?"

I had to admit I hadn't, and I'd bet she didn't either. What she thought was a ghost was probably nothing more than a shadow. "I'm going to have a doctor come look at you and see if there's something he can give you to make you feel better."

"Thank ya, Miss Olivia."

I was glad she didn't argue with me, but I assumed it was most likely because she didn't have the strength to. "I'll be back soon," I said, closing the door softly behind me.

When I went back to the kitchen, Theresa immediately handed me the plate of sausage and eggs that she'd been keeping warm for me. I took a few bites, then said, "I know you don't think a doctor will do any good for Molly, but it's worth a try, even if only to give her something to make her more comfortable. Don't you agree?"

Theresa nodded, and so did the other women. After I finished eating, I asked, "Have you seen Jaxon this morning?"

Dottie stopped loading the dishwasher and wiped her wet hands on her apron. "He was here a few minutes ago when ya were upstairs with Molly. Had somethin' to eat, and then said he was goin' to be in the study makin' some phone calls."

"He wanted to schedule some newspaper ads for the openin' of the bed-and-breakfast," Theresa added.

"Thank you. That was delicious," I said, handing my plate to Dottie.

Sure enough, I found Jaxon in the study, sitting at my grandfather's old rolltop desk.

He flashed me a grin when I came in. "Good morning."

My cheeks warmed as I recalled the heady sensation of his lips on mine, and I hoped the kisses that we'd shared wouldn't make things awkward between us. "About yesterday," I began, but he quickly cut me off.

"What about it?" Amusement flickered in his eyes.

I licked my lips nervously. "It was a very emotional day for me."

"I know." He sat back in the chair, leisurely stretching his long legs.

Jax wasn't going to make this easy for me. "I don't want what happened between us to interfere with work or make things weird or uncomfortable."

His brows shot up. "Why would it?"

I shrugged, not quite sure how to explain what I was feeling.

"Look, Liv, nothing's changed. We shared a couple kisses—very nice ones, I might add. But that's all there was to it. There's nothing to worry about. You were upset, I was there. End of story. So are we good?"

I blinked quickly in shock. I hadn't expected him to say *that*, but at least I knew exactly where I stood with him. Nowhere. What happened yesterday had been just a brief moment of passion. One that he probably had with lots of women.

"Yes, we're fine." I shifted my gaze away from his penetrating stare. "Molly's sick. Do you think Dr. Becker would come out to have a look at her?"

"I'm sure he would." He opened the desk drawer and pulled out the notebook where the wireless network key was written. "What do you think's wrong with her?" he asked as he flipped through the pages.

"I don't know. Maybe one of the casseroles from the funeral didn't agree with her. Although, the staff thinks it's the curse."

His expression changed, but I couldn't read it.

"Here you go," he said, handing me the book.

Our fingers brushed as I took it from his hand, and a tingle ran up my neck. "Thanks."

"Jess asked me to go into town with her to meet with the interior designer. Guess they're going to be picking the material for the guest rooms. You don't mind, do you?"

A strange feeling settled in my stomach. Could it be jealousy? "No, of course not. Why would I?"

"I don't know. Just checking, boss. Wouldn't want to do anything to upset you."

"As long as you both do what I hired you to do, I don't care how it gets done." When I left the room, I could tell he was staring at my back. Good. I was glad that I'd gotten the point across that what happened between us yesterday didn't mean anything to me either.

Although, I might have fooled him, I couldn't fool myself. I was afraid I was falling hard for Jaxon.

~ecencao~

IT WAS SURPRISING how quickly Dr. Becker came out for Molly. I doubted there was a doctor anywhere in Boston who'd make a house call, never mind doing so within a few hours.

After his examination, I asked, "Is she going to be all right?"

"I believe so. Could be a virus or a touch of food poisoning. It'll just have to run its course. I did give her something to help with the nausea, though. I'll be back to check on her in a few days. If you need me before then, just give a call." His calm manner was reassuring.

"Thank you so much, Dr. Becker."

"My pleasure."

After showing him out, I went back upstairs to see Molly and was glad that to find her sitting up in bed.

"Aren't you happy I had the doctor come out, if for no other reason than to put your mind at ease? No ghosts. No curse. Just a regular illness that should be gone in a few days."

She smiled a little, but I could tell she wasn't totally convinced. "Thank ya for everythin', Miss Olivia. I hate to have been such a bother."

"It's no bother. Like I told you before, I just want you to get well."

Her eyes fluttered, an indication that she needed more sleep.

"Is there anything I can get you before I leave? Something to drink, maybe?"

"Dat would be nice."

"Okay. I'll be right back." Downstairs in the kitchen, the choices were orange juice or sweet tea.

I didn't think the juice would be good for her stomach, so I poured her a glass of the tea. When I went back up to her room, she was already asleep, so I put the drink on her nightstand.

After leaving her, I went into my grandfather's study to go over the stack of bills that had been piling up. I had no idea if we were anywhere near on budget with all the projects we had going on at once. The bed-and-breakfast was scheduled to open next month, and I hoped that nothing would come up to derail it. As I went over everything, I realized that we hadn't hired an electrician to put in the additional outlets that were needed in the guest rooms.

I opened the desk drawer, running my hand along the back of it in search of grandfather's notebook, thinking he might have an electrician listed in it. He seemed to have everything else.

When I pulled it out, I half expected to drag out his journal as well. However, that was nowhere to be found. Who would take my grandfather's diary? Who would even know it was in that drawer? I remembered earlier, when Jaxon took out the notebook to get me Dr. Becker's phone number. He might have known the journal was there, but would he take it and why? I made a mental note to ask him when he got back from his trip to town with Jessica.

Chapter Nine

I SPENT THE entire day in the study going over expenses and making appointments for last-minute things we'd forgotten, such as the electrician.

As the day wore on, I kept glancing at the clock, wondering where Jaxon and Jessica were and kicking myself for having told Jax I didn't care what they did as long as their work got done.

I knew one thing, though: I wasn't going to let them know that their being gone so long bothered me.

When Theresa came in to ask if I wanted dinner, I told her to just make me a plate and stick it in the refrigerator so I could eat it later. It wasn't until nine p.m. that I made my way into the kitchen. I'd just finished eating when Jaxon and Jess came strolling in. They seemed to be in a great mood, laughing and chatting.

"What an absolutely perfect day," Jessica said. "You wouldn't believe the stunning fabrics Nancy showed us. It was so difficult to decide what to use where, but I think you'll be happy with our choices, Liv. At least I hope you'll be."

"I'm sure they're fine. That's why I put you in charge." I went over to the sink and rinsed off my plate and then stuck it in the dishwasher. "If you'll excuse me, I'm going to bed. It's been a long and tiring day." As I was about to leave, I turned to Jaxon. "You wouldn't happen to have my grandfather's journal, would you? It was in his desk drawer, and now it's gone."

He crossed his arms over his chest. "I didn't even know it was in there. What about you, Jess? Any idea where it might be?"

She had her back was to us, as she was on her way out of the kitchen. "Nope. Sorry."

When she was gone, Jax said, "We wound up going to New Orleans for dinner, and I made an appointment for you for tomorrow with Lily Dewitt. She's a well-known psychic who also does past life regression."

"What time?" I asked, annoyed that he would do that without checking with me first.

"One p.m."

I shook my head. "I have an electrician coming to install additional outlets in the guest rooms at that time."

"And you have to be there when he does that?" he asked with determined firmness.

I rolled my eyes. "No, I guess not."

"Good. I'll have Gerard handle the electrician. See, there's no reason we can't go."

His smug smile irked me. "Fine. I'll see you tomorrow."

When I was up in my room, I'd wished I'd stood my ground and not agreed to go with Jax to see the psychic. All this talk of ghosts and curses and past lives was really starting to get to me. And by going to the appointment tomorrow, I'd only be encouraging more of it. But I never went back on my word, and I wasn't about to do so now. I'd go and get it over with, and then put an end to all this foolishness once and for all.

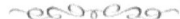

As WE DROVE down Dauphine Street, there was something about it that made me feel like I'd been there before. The buildings with their elaborate wrought iron railings and potted plants hanging from second-floor balconies seemed so familiar.

Jaxon pulled up in front of one with red shutters and a black front door. "Why don't you go ahead in while I find somewhere to park? I don't want you to be late for your appointment."

While I didn't relish the idea of going inside alone, I knew he was right. It was one o'clock now.

"It'll be fine," he said, sensing my hesitation.

I got out of the car and watched him pull down the street before going inside. As I entered the building, a bell above the door jingled, announcing my arrival. I had a weird sense of déjà vu. The place smelled of an odd combination of candles and incense. A small, thin woman who couldn't have been more than five feet tall came out of a back room.

"Hello, I'm Lily Dewitt," she said, offering me her hand.

I slid my hand into hers. "It's nice to meet you, Lily. I'm Olivia Lockwood."

"I know who you are." The way she said it made me think she meant it in a way other than because I had an appointment with her.

"Jax tells me you've been experiencing some past life memories." For some reason I got the impression she knew Jaxon and that he hadn't just found her at random.

"I'm not sure what they are. That's why I'm here."

"Of course, my dear. I can help you with that. These memories can be quite startling when they first appear. Come with me." She walked toward the back room.

I hesitated a moment before following, wishing Jax would hurry up and get here.

"There's no need to be nervous," she said, opening the door and stepping inside the room.

I went in too, my gaze quickly taking in my surroundings. The first thing I noticed was the plush white leather recliner. Beside it was a small wooden table and chair. On the table were two candles and an MP3 player.

"Make yourself comfortable," she said, pointing to the leather recliner.

Once I was lying back in the chair, she sat at

the table and turned on the player. Soft, soothing music filled the room. "What I'd like you to do is close your eyes and relax. I'm going to take you to a higher level of consciousness, and once you're there, you're going to go back to the origin or root cause of your problem." She paused for a moment so the only sound was that of the music. "I want you to take a couple of deep breaths, Livvy, concentrating solely on the rhythm of your breath, then imagine a beautiful white light encompassing your entire body, beginning at your feet and moving up all the way to the top of your head. You're in another dimension now, another time. Can you tell me where you are?"

Images whirred past me—women in long dresses, men in waistcoats, Federal-style rowhouses, and gas streetlamps. "Yes, I'm in Boston." My voice sounded small and far away.

"Do you know what year it is?"

"It's 1851."

"Tell me what you see and hear."

"It's noisy. There are lots of carriages. I need to cross the street, but I don't want to get run down, so I'm waitin' for a break."

"Who are you?"

"My name is Jane, and I'm a seamstress."

"Do you have a husband and children?"

A tear ran down my cheek, and it took a moment for me to answer. "No. I'm alone."

"Why is that?"

"The only man I've ever loved is in Louisiana. I haven't seen him in twenty years. I don't even know if he remembers me. He was a man of wealth and privilege, and I was just a slave, though my father was the master of a fine plantation."

"And you've carried that pain with you all these years?"

"Yes."

"You have to release it, Jane. Do you understand?"

"Yes."

"How are you going to do that?"

I stirred uneasily in the chair. "I don't know. But I think I see him. He's walkin' toward me." A gamut of emotions raged through me. "No, it can't be him. Here in Boston? What will I say to him? Do I look all right?"

"You look fine, Jane. You can't run away. You have to speak to him. You realize that, don't you?"

"Yes." I bit my lip nervously.

"Good. Take a deep breath, and meet him halfway."

Chapter Ten

Boston, Massachusetts, 1851

As I STOOD at the edge of the brick sidewalk, I couldn't believe my eyes. A tall, muscular man with golden hair was crossing the street and headed in my direction. About halfway across, he spotted me and froze.

I let out a little scream as a carriage just missed him. My heart was thundering so fast, I felt sure its pounding had to be visible through my dress. When he reached me, I thought I might actually stop breathing.

Up close, his hair had streaks of gray peppered throughout, and there were wrinkles at the corners of his eyes and mouth, but he was as handsome as I remembered.

"Jane, is that really you? I can't believe it." His gaze scanned me from head to toe.

"You're in Boston?"

"On business. I leave in the mornin'." He pointed to the hotel to the right of us. "I'm stayin' there."

A cold November wind blew, and he took hold of my arm and led me into the lobby.

"Do you have a few minutes to catch up?"

I was only going home to my tiny, dank apartment. I had all the time he wanted. "How's Sarah?" I asked, taking a seat in one of the wing-backed chairs.

He sat next to me, not answering right away. "She died twenty years ago, shortly after you left."

I swallowed hard, trying to fathom Sarah being gone. "And my ma?" My mouth trembled, fearing the worst for her as well.

A little smile lit his face. "She's fine. Still tough and strong as an ox."

I leaned back in the chair and let out a small sigh of relief, although that was short-lived.

"I wish I could say the same for your father, though," he added. "He's quite ill, Jane."

Sorrow ripped at my heart, but I fought hard to keep my emotions at bay. There would be time to mourn later, when I was alone. My gaze shifted from his face to his left hand and the gold band he wore.

"You're married?" I asked, swallowing the lump that had formed in my throat.

"Yes," he replied softly, his gaze traveling over my hand and the lack of jewelry on it.

"Any children?" I asked.

"One son."

"You must be happy." It wasn't a question. It was a statement.

Uncertainty crept into his expression. "I guess that depends how you define happy." There was no mistaking the clenching of his jaw. "Are you?"

I plucked at my skirt, not quite sure how to answer. "I no longer live in fear. And I have a job I like." We both knew I was evading the question.

My eyes opened wide when he reached into the pocket of his overcoat and pulled out my spinel pendant. "I've carried this with me all these years," he said, almost to himself. "Somehow, havin' it with me made me feel close to you." His eyes locked with mine, his gaze penetrating so deep, it was as if he wanted to look into my soul. "You're the only woman I've ever loved, Jane." He held the necklace out to me, and it shimmered with a magnificent fire beneath the lights of the chandelier above us.

My fingers touched the cold, smooth stone and then the warmth of his hand, and I felt like my body was on fire. "Keep it," I said, tucking my hands back into the folds of my gown. "I don't need it now."

He looked at me questioningly and then nodded as he placed the necklace back into his pocket. "Jane, I wish there was some way..." His voice trailed off as he struggled for the words to express his feelings.

I reached over and caressed his cheek with the back of my hand. "We'll be together again, someday...somewhere. I promise." I recited the pledge he'd said to me that day so long ago before I made my escape to freedom.

One tear rolled from his eye onto my hand, and I didn't need anything else from him. The knowledge that our love had survived was enough. I turned and left the hotel without looking back. A peacefulness had settled over me, and I would carry it with me until my death.

Chapter Eleven

Present Day – Louisiana

THE WHITE LIGHT that had surrounded me was growing smaller and dimmer, until it was completely gone.

"Olivia, can you hear me?" a woman asked.

I nodded, not quite sure where I was.

"I need you to come back to the present now. You're at peace, and you can live this lifetime with the issues of your past resolved. Take a deep breath, and let it out slowly."

I did as she said.

"Another," she advised. "Now open your eyes."

When I opened them, it took a minute to bring the room into focus and for me to remember the woman talking to me was Lily Dewitt.

She turned off the MP3 player and smiled at me. "How do you feel?"

I blinked with bafflement. "At ease."

Her smile broadened in approval. "Good."

"So those really were past life memories?"

"Most definitely."

"Will I have more of them?"

"Probably not, since you were able to work through your problem."

A part of me was sad that I might not get to visit my life as Jane again. And then a thought dawned on me, and my pulse began to thrum. "Since I've lived other lifetimes, does that mean Ellis might have too? Could he be here now as someone else?"

Her eyes shone with understanding. "You'd like that, wouldn't you?"

"I've never had a serious relationship. Not one that I could commit to. I've always felt like I was waiting for that special guy to walk into my life. I know now that I've been waiting for Ellis."

Lily got up and came over to me, taking my hand in hers. "There's a high probability that you'll have several lifetimes with the people you're closest to, but this may not be one of them."

A dull ache formed in my chest, and an acute sense of loss spread over me. But I was unwilling to give up hope. "How will I know if he's here?"

"One way or another, you'll find each other."

I thought about that for a moment before asking, "Will I know him right away?"

"It might take time. You'll feel drawn to him for no apparent reason. But if you want proof, look for a scar or birthmark that Ellis had. They carry over from lifetime to lifetime. When you see it, a picture should form in your mind, and you'll know it's him." Lily got up and went over to the window, staring out into a pretty little courtyard, then she turned to face me. "The same is true for your spinel pendant."

I reached for my necklace, rubbing my finger over the stone. "How do you mean?"

"Ellis will recognize it and know that you're Jane."

"My mother said it would protect me from danger. Is that true?"

"An amulet is a very powerful object. It's used to protect and repel negative energy. However, it will only work for the person who wears it, and it's charged with a specific act of protection."

"Like a centuries-old curse?" I asked, thinking of how even today evil Tucker Sheldon had a hold on those living in Turnberry.

"Precisely." She looked at her watch and then walked over to the door. "I'm so glad I could help you today, my dear."

"Me too. Thank you." When I left the room, I found Jaxon out front, flipping through a magazine.

"All set?" he asked when he saw me.

"Yes." I thanked Lily again before leaving, and we both waved to her on the way out.

"How about we get something to eat before we head home?" Jaxon flashed me his fabulous smile.

That little spike of jealousy returned when I thought of how he had dinner here in the city last night with Jess. I knew it was ridiculous to feel that way. After all, there was nothing going on between us. Our kiss was just a kiss, nothing more. He'd made that perfectly clear. Besides, I didn't want to spend any more time developing feelings for a man who wasn't right for me. If Ellis was here somewhere, I needed to find him.

I WAS QUITE impressed with Jaxon's choice of restaurants. Antoine's opened in 1840 and was still owned and operated by relatives of the original founder. Sitting there in one of its charming and beautiful dining rooms took me back in time, quite appropriate considering the events that led up to us coming there.

We ordered the Chateaubriand for two and a bottle of red wine. While we waited for dinner, Jaxon gave me a brief history lesson on New Orleans—a place of second chances.

"So I hope you understand a little better now why the people here believe as they do," he said before taking a sip of his wine.

"Indeed."

"And what about you? Did your visit with Lily Dewitt make you a believer?"

"I have to admit that I do believe that what I've been experiencing were events from another lifetime. There's just no other explanation. But as far as believing in ghosts and a curse, I'm not sure I've come that far."

He took another sip of wine. The dancing candlelight from the table's centerpiece, cast a warm glow over him, making him even more attractive. "That's okay. You're making progress. In time, you'll come around."

Those words were similar to what Kelly had said, and I suddenly felt homesick. "A good friend of mine said something very much like that to me before I left Boston."

"Must be a wise friend."

"She is."

"Do you miss home?"

"With everything that's been going on here, I've hardly had a chance to think about it until now, and I must say, thinking about Kelly does make me miss my life there, as dull as it might have been." My voice wavered with the brilliance of his look.

"I'm sorry. I didn't mean to make you sad."

"That's okay. It was bound to happen at some point."

"But not tonight. Tonight we're celebrating." He raised his glass to me.

"We are?" I said, lifting mine. "What are we celebrating?"

"You...becoming one of us."

The rest of the evening was spent discussing the bed-and-breakfast and how close we were coming to the grand opening.

When we left the restaurant, Jaxon placed his arm across my shoulders as we walked toward the car. Once we were seated inside it, he leaned toward me.

"I had a really nice time tonight," he said, his breath warm on my cheek.

"I did too."

I don't know if it was the wine or the fact that we had this undeniable connection, despite us both not wanting to admit it, but somehow I wound up in his arms, and once again his firm lips were on mine. His kiss was demanding and urgent, and I was shocked at how I responded to him. His lips seared a path down my neck and shoulders, setting my body aflame with desire, and then back up to my eagerly awaiting mouth.

I lost track of time. It wasn't until a group of noisy teenagers walked past the car that our lips parted.

During the ride home, neither one of us spoke, both lost in our own thoughts. What did tonight mean? Anything? Or would Jaxon brush our kisses off again? I supposed I would find out soon enough.

Back at Turnberry, the house was quiet. Everyone was either asleep or in their rooms. After a polite good night, we retired to ours as well, leaving me not knowing what to make of that man.

I couldn't fall asleep. My thoughts were a jumbled mess, so instead of fighting it, I turned on my bedside lamp and began to read Ellis's journal.

November, 1851

After seeing Jane in Boston, I couldn't get her out of my head. All the way back to Louisiana, she was the only thing I thought of. I know I should have been wondering how my wife and son were doing, but Jane, never far from my thoughts before, was front and center now—demanding all my attention.

Although I was ecstatic to have run into her and discover that she was alive and well, dispelling once and for all my fears of what might have happened to her, the other part of me—the part that had fought so hard over these twenty years to maintain some kind of contentment, if not happiness, knew those days were gone. Jane's face, her touch, her smell, was burned into my soul, and would remain there forever.

The next day, I went to Turnberry, not caring that I was unwelcome. I was doing this for Jane. William deserved to know that she had made it north and had obtained the freedom that she'd craved. He also deserved to have a part of her. I gave him her necklace. Like Jane, I no longer needed it. Everything that I held dear was seared upon my heart, now and forever.

That was the last entry Ellis had made. A painful knot twisted inside me. I closed the journal and turned out the light. At some point before dawn, I fell asleep.

Chapter Twelve

As I HEADED downstairs for breakfast, I wondered, after last night if things would be weird and awkward with Jaxon.

I need not have worried, though, because as I entered the kitchen, he rushed by me with a blueberry muffin in one hand and a cup of coffee in the other, and said cheerfully, "Good morning, Liv. Busy day today. The restoration on the slave quarters and the rest of the buildings out back should be completed this afternoon. When you have a chance, come have a look."

"Great. I will."

He flashed me his awesome smile and disappeared down the hall. After he was gone, I glanced around the kitchen, expecting to find Molly back at work, but she was nowhere to be seen.

"Theresa, where's Molly?" I asked.

"She got really sick durin' the night, Miss Olivia," she replied grimly.

I raced into the pantry and up the back stairs toward her bedroom. Without bothering to knock, I flung open the door. Molly lay on the bed, her face ashen.

"What happened?" I asked, going to stand beside the bed. "I'd thought after seeing Dr. Becker that you were doing better."

"I thought so too." Her voice was small and weak. "Guess, ya were wrong, Miss Olivia, and it really was the curse out to get me." Sobs racked her thin body.

Something weird was going on, and I doubted it had anything to do with a curse, but Molly did, and it wouldn't help her condition to have her hysterical because she thought she was going to die.

I reached around my neck and undid the clasp to my spinel pendant, taking off the necklace and then handing it to Molly. "Keep this with you. It'll protect you from danger."

"Really?"

"Yes, it's an amulet made especially for that

purpose."

A hopeful gleam lit her tired eyes.

"I know you don't think he can help, but I'm going to call Dr. Becker. I'll be back soon."

She clutched my necklace, and I was glad I had something to give her hope.

After I left her, I ran up to my room to call the doctor, but got his voice mail, so I left a message explaining that Molly's condition had worsened. While I waited for a callback, I turned on my laptop and did a search on her symptoms. I could barely believe what popped up—arsenic poisoning. The tasteless white powder mimics the symptoms of a natural illness, causing severe gastric distress, vomiting, skin irritations, hair loss, and eventually heart failure.

Prickles of fear crept up the back of my neck as I remembered the baggie of white powder that had fallen out of the kitchen cabinet when I went to take down a pitcher. I knew I could be jumping to conclusions and that could have just been a bag of sugar, and Molly's illness might not be from arsenic at all, but if I was right... Well, the thought was beyond comprehension. And then I recalled how sick I'd been... I was getting way ahead of myself, but I couldn't help it. All kinds of crazy thoughts started to pop into my head. Who would do such a thing? And why would anyone want to hurt Molly? Or me, for that matter? It didn't make sense, but then nothing that had been happening here since I arrived did.

I hurried down to the kitchen to look for that baggie, but after searching all the cabinets, it was nowhere to be found. I was trying to think of where else I could look when Jessica walked in. She went over to the counter and took a banana from a basket of fruit. As she started to peel it, I said, "Have you heard Molly's taken a turn for the worse?"

She took a bite of the fruit, chewing slowly, and then said, "No, I didn't know that. What's wrong with her, do you know?"

"Seems like some kind of mysterious illness or maybe arsenic poisoning." I knew I was taking a chance saying anything to her, but if someone was poisoning people, I needed to do what I could to try to find out who that might be.

She put her banana down on the counter and stared at me. "Seriously? Arsenic?" Her face was ashen. "Do you think it's in the water? Could we all be in danger?"

I wasn't about to tell her that I didn't think it had anything to do with the water or that I'd found a baggie full of some kind of powdery white substance. "I don't know. I'm going to have some testing done, just to be sure, though."

"Good idea. Let me know what you find out." She finished her banana and then left the kitchen.

About mid-afternoon, Dr. Becker came by to reexamine Molly. When we were alone, I told him of my concerns.

"I think it's a little farfetched to think that someone would intentionally poison her, but I'll have some blood work done, just to rule it out. Regardless, though, she needs to be in the hospital. I'll call for an ambulance to come pick her up."

Before Molly left, I tried to reassure her that the hospital was the best place for her. I could tell she didn't believe that, but thankfully, she didn't put up a fuss.

"Thank ya for lettin' me borrow this." She handed me the spinel pendant.

"Don't you want to take it with you?" I asked.

"It doesn't seem to be doin' any good. But I appreciate yar attempt to help."

My heart went out to her, and I prayed that she'd get well. After she left, I remembered that I'd told Jaxon I would take a look at the refurbished buildings, and I headed out back. As I walked through the French parterre garden, I was lost in thought, trying to wrap my head around what might be going on at the house.

I went through the white swinging gate and was almost at the slave quarters when I heard voices from behind one of the old cypress trees. It took a moment for me to realize it was Jess.

"I think Livvy might be on to us," she said, her voice dripping with venom.

"What makes you think that?"

It was a man's voice. Jax? It was too muffled to know for sure, but who else could it be? My heart pounded, and I was frozen with fear.

"Because she was talking about arsenic poisoning," Jessica replied. "You should have seen the way she was looking at me. I'm telling you, she might have seen me put it in the sweet tea."

I clasped my hand over my mouth to silence my gasp. I'd given Molly a glass of sweet tea the other day. They'd been poisoning her, and probably me too. I thought back to how I'd had a whole glass of that tea, and later that night was when I'd gotten so violently ill. How could my cousin do that? And Jaxon? How could I have been so wrong about him? I must be a terrible judge of character to think that I was falling in love with someone capable of murder.

I needed to get out of here. If they saw me, who knew what they would do? I took a step back, but my foot crunched on a twig.

"Did you hear that?" Jess asked, peering out from behind the tree. Our eyes met, and what I saw in hers was pure hatred. "Livvy's here," she spat.

I wanted to run back to the house, but they'd intercept me if I went in that direction, so I headed toward the river instead. Footsteps rang out behind me. I ran as fast as I could, but they were closing in on me.

I expected to feel arms around my throat at any second now. Instead, someone yelled stop and then there was a loud thud.

I had no idea what was going on behind me, and I wasn't about to turn around to find out. I just kept running and running, like I had from Tucker's men, centuries ago. I came to the spot where I'd tripped over the log. Only this time, luckily, there was nothing there to make me fall.

"Livvy," Jaxon yelled, from not far behind. "I'm not going to hurt you. I'd never hurt you."

How big a fool did he think I was? I might have been taken in by him before, but I sure wasn't about to be again. I should have known better. He was a Clairmont, after all, and there was good reason to fear them. His great-great-great-grandfather had wanted me dead, and now he did too.

"We'll be together again, someday... somewhere. I promise."

Had I really just heard Ellis's haunting words? I must've slowed down some, because Jaxon caught me around the waist, bringing me to an abrupt halt.

"What did you say?" I gasped.

"I'll love you forever, Jane. Nothing will ever change that." He pressed his mouth to mine.

His kiss sent spirals of ecstasy through me. "Ellis?" I whispered.

With one hand, he unbuttoned his shirt, letting it drop off his left shoulder to expose a birthmark in the exact spot where Tucker had stabbed him centuries ago. That horrible scene replayed in my mind.

"It *is* you. I can't believe it," I cried, and then

his mouth was on mine again, moist, firm, and demanding a response. As I kissed him back, I thought I was being transported through time on a soft and wispy cloud, then everything seemed to stand still, and I realized we were at the edge of the mighty Mississippi River.

When our lips finally parted, I stared into his gorgeous blue-gray eyes. "How long have you known you were Ellis?"

"For a while. I started experiencing my past life years ago."

"And when did you know I was Jane?"

He smiled. "As soon as I saw you, and your necklace confirmed it."

My brow furrowed. "But you never let on. You never said a word."

"Lily advised me not to. She said you needed to come to terms with things in your own time and in your own way."

"So you did know Lily. She wasn't just someone you found at random."

He laughed. "No, I've seen Lily many times. In fact, my mother referred her to me."

The mention of his mother reminded me of my own family and my despicable cousin. "Where's

Jess, and why were you conspiring with her?" Although all my instincts told me there was no reason to fear him, I knew there were many more secrets he hadn't told me.

He held me snugly in his arms. "It's a long story. Are you sure you want to hear it now?"

I gazed up at his handsome face and thought I detected a flicker in his intense eyes. "I have all the time it takes to tell it."

"I wasn't conspiring with Jessica, I was trying to find out what she was up to. I knew that when Asa as much as cut her out of his will and left everything to you, she'd be out to get you. I just didn't think she'd resort to murder. Jess has always been only about Jess, and I knew she was unscrupulous...but using arsenic... Liv, that's insane."

I shook my head, still not sure why she would want to hurt Molly. "But why was she trying to poison a kitchen worker?"

"My guess is she was trying to cover her tracks. If Molly died from some mysterious illness, then it wouldn't seem suspicious when you became sick shortly after that. And of course, many people would just assume it was the curse. No one would ever suspect poisoning."

"How did you?"

"I didn't. Not until the other day. I thought she might try to find a way to get you to leave here before the six months were up. But even with that, I figured she'd need help to execute such a plan."

"So it wasn't you I heard her talking to behind the cypress tree?"

"No." A look came over his face that I'd never seen before. "When I went with her to New Orleans to look at fabrics for the guest rooms, I thought that would be the perfect opportunity to try to get her to open up to me. Maybe see if I could find out if she was involved with someone." He took a deep breath before continuing, and it was apparent this was painful for him. "When we were at dinner, she went to use the ladies' room. As she got up from the table, her purse fell off the back of the chair and onto the floor. A baggie full of some kind of white substance fell out. She doesn't use extra sugar in her drinks and I'd never known her to use drugs of any kind, so I was curious to find out what it was. She quickly pushed it back into her handbag. But a little had spilled onto the floor, so when she was gone, I scooped it into a napkin. And when you were with Lily, I took it to a lab to have it tested. I got the results this afternoon when I was finishing up with the restorations in the slave quarters."

"It *was* arsenic," I said flatly.

He nodded. "I immediately called the police. I was waiting for them to arrive when you ran by like your hair was on fire."

"So it was an officer who yelled stop?"

"Yes, before tackling my stepfather."

My body stiffened in shock, and I let out a gasp. "What?"

A look of tired sadness passed over his features. "I not only have to tell my mom that her husband was having an affair, but that he's also a criminal."

"Oh, Jax. I am so, so sorry." Pain squeezed my heart as I thought of how difficult it would be for him to do that.

"Thank you." He kissed me softly, then asked, "Are you ready to go back to the house?"

I nodded. As we walked, I tried to process everything that had happened, and I was sure Jaxon was trying to figure out the best way to break the terrible news to his mom.

When we reached the mansion, Jess and Nigel

were in handcuffs. A police officer walked up to us.

"I'm sorry about this," he said to me. "It's no way to welcome you into our town. I knew Asa. He was a good man. Luckily, Jaxon took it upon himself to do some investigating, or we could have had a real tragedy on our hands. We need more citizens like him."

"I was just doing what had to be done to protect those I love." His eyes locked with mine.

After Jessica and Nigel were taken away and all the police had left, Jaxon said, "I should spend the night at Clairmont."

"Of course. I know you're worried about your mom."

Fatigue settled in rings under his eyes. "Are you going to be okay?"

I stroked his cheek. "Of course. I have Gerard and the rest of the staff. It's not like I'll be at Turnberry alone. Besides, now that Jess is gone, there's nothing to worry about."

He kissed me tenderly, then headed over to the neighboring plantation.

Inside the house, the back hall smelled of onions and spices. The kitchen staff was busily preparing dinner. Theresa was at the stove, stirring a big pot of gumbo. When I entered, she spun around and then ran over to me, giving me a hug.

"Oh, Miss Olivia. We're so glad ya're okay. We can't believe what Miss Jessica tried to do. And dat Nigel Harris. What a horrible man he turned out to be."

I hugged her back. News sure traveled fast.

"You must be starvin'." She took hold of my arm and led me over to a stool. "Sit down and let me fix ya somethin' to eat."

Without waiting for my reply, she was at the stove, getting me a bowl of gumbo. When she set it down in front of me, she said, "I'm so worried about Molly. Is she goin' to be okay?"

I wished I could say for sure, but I just didn't know. "She's in good hands at the hospital. They're doing everything they can for her. But she can use our prayers. Let's not talk of anything negative tonight, all right?"

"Of course."

"I plan to visit her tomorrow, and I'll be sure to let you know if there's any improvement."

After I finished eating, I headed upstairs to my room. On the way, I stopped at the bedroom that Jessica had used. I didn't want anything of hers in this house, so I started to pack up her things. When I finished putting the clothes that were in the closet into her suitcase, I began to empty out the dresser. The only thing left was the nightstand. I opened the drawer, expecting to find a novel or two. Instead, I discovered my grandfather's journal.

I gritted my teeth as I stuck it in my pocket, saying a silent prayer of thanks that Jessica had been arrested. That woman was pure evil.

I had Gerard take her suitcases downstairs and put them on the back porch so that in the morning, he could drop them off at Uncle Paul's house.

Night had fallen by the time I headed back to my room. The darkened hall was eerily quiet with everyone gone. As I was about to open my door, from the corner of my eye, I saw a shadowy figure dart by. My hand froze on the knob as I scanned the hallway, but nothing was there. Had I just seen the ghost of Tucker Sheldon?

With my heart racing, I bolted inside my room, locking the door behind me. I stood there for a few minutes, trying to find a logical explanation for what I had just seen, but I couldn't find one. Yet, despite my meeting with Lily Dewitt and my past life experience, I still wasn't sure I believed in ghosts and curses. So what dashed by me, then? Could I have imagined it? I was exhausted, and my nerves were shot. That seemed the most probable, or at least what I hoped to be, the explanation.

Before I undressed, I took my grandfather's journal out of my pocket and tossed it on the bed, sure it would make for interesting reading, and hopefully help me fall asleep. If only Jaxon were here... Having him down the hall would've offered the comfort I needed right now. But he'd done the right thing by going to Clairmont. No doubt, his mother needed him more than I did tonight. I tried to imagine what it would be like to learn of all the horrible things her husband had been up to, but I couldn't. And I was so thankful that I'd never have to worry about being in her position someday. I'd finally found the man I'd been waiting for, and I knew that he'd never deceive me.

With that happy thought, I climbed into bed and began reading about my grandfather's life.

Chapter Thirteen

Yawning, I turned another page of my grandfather's journal. I'd learned so much about him, and I was only halfway through. I wished now, more than ever, that I'd had the chance to spend time with him when I'd been growing up.

After reading another twenty pages or so, I came to some entries that chased all thoughts of sleep away. Shortly after marrying Jaxon's mom, Nigel approached Asa about selling Turnberry to the Clairmont's—that was twelve years ago. They'd had a terrible fight, and Nigel warned Grandfather that he'd be sorry. It wasn't long after that that Nigel was caught having an affair with Cammy, the woman who died shortly after my mom and with similar symptoms.

I broke out in a cold sweat as an awful thought popped into my head. What if my mom didn't die from the flu or some other illness? Cammy either. What if they'd both been poisoned?

I slammed the journal shut, then ran my hands over my face. Coming here had been a mistake. Maybe this place really was cursed.

I swung my legs over the side of the bed and started to pace the floor. *What to do! What to do!* The bed-and-breakfast was going to open in a few weeks, but I didn't know if I could last until then, let alone six months. Next, my thoughts drifted to Jaxon. What about him? He'd be devastated. We'd finally found each other. Thoughts swirled around in my head, only confusing me more. I needed to talk to someone who could shed some common sense on my dilemma.

I grabbed my cellphone off the nightstand and checked the time. Not quite midnight. My dad was a night owl. Most likely he'd be awake. Without further hesitation, I dialed home.

He answered right away. "Livvy Luv, I've been thinking about you. How are things?"

"Oh, Dad! So much has happened, I don't even know where to begin. Most of it is crazy stuff. I think I want to come home."

I heard his sharp intake of breath, and then there was a long pause before he spoke. "You know what I always say about making rash decisions."

"They usually don't turn out to be the right ones."

"Exactly. And isn't the bed-and-breakfast due to open soon?"

"In two weeks."

"You've put an awful lot of work into it, Liv, to give up now."

"Dad, you don't know what I've been through."

"Look, I have an idea. It doesn't sound like what's been happening there is something that should be discussed over the phone. Why don't you try to get a flight home tomorrow? Spend a few days in Boston. We'll talk things over and decide then what's best for you."

Relief spread through me. As always, my dad had come to my rescue. "Thanks, Dad. That's exactly what I need to do."

"Don't worry, Liv. Once things are put in the proper perspective, they have a way of working out."

"Good night, Dad. Love you."

"Love you too, sweetie."

When I hung up the phone, I felt much better. Just the thought of going home helped me fall asleep. Although I did wind up keeping the light on. That incident in the hall had unnerved me more than I cared to admit.

THE FIRST THING I did when I woke was book a flight home. I was able to get one for late afternoon, allowing time for a quick visit to the hospital to see Molly.

"How are you feeling?" I asked, pulling up a chair next to the bed.

A small smile brightened her face. "Believe it or not, better. It's too soon to know if there'll be any long-term effects, but at least I'm not goin' to die."

"I'm so sorry this happened to you." I squeezed her hand. "I feel responsible."

"Please don't, Miss Olivia. Ya couldn't have known what those two were up to. Besides, everyone was so happy that yar grandfather left Turnberry to ya and dat ya're turnin' it into a bed-

and-breakfast."

"Even with Tucker Sheldon's curse?"

"It's home, and I love it. Nowhere's perfect." She sat up straighter in bed. "Does this mean ya're a believer now?"

I shrugged. "I don't know about that. But I do wonder if there's something going on in the house."

"Miss Olivia, ya saw the ghost, didn't ya?"

A shiver of recollection ran through me. "I saw something last night, or at least thought I did. But let me make one thing clear: I don't believe for a second that any of us are in danger any longer. Real live people were responsible for that." I stood and pushed the chair back to where I'd found it. "I'm leaving for Boston later this afternoon. Just for a few days. If you're still in here when I return, and not back at work"—I winked—"I'll come visit again."

"Have a good trip."

"I will." I waved good-bye as I walked out the door.

When I got back to Turnberry, Jaxon was in the study, on the phone, taking a reservation for our opening weekend.

"I heard you went to see Molly," he said after

he hung up.

"I did. I just came from there."

He walked around the rolltop desk and wrapped his arms around me. "How is she?"

"Much better than I expected. It was great to see her spirits up."

He pulled me closer so that his mouth was just inches from mine. "And how are you?"

"I don't know."

He pulled back a little so that he could look straight into my eyes. "I don't like the sound of that. What's going on?"

"Let's go somewhere private to talk."

"How about a walk?"

"Perfect."

Somehow we always seemed to wind up at the riverbank, and that seemed appropriate for today's conversation.

As I stood there looking out at the water, I struggled with how to tell Jaxon what was on my mind. "So much has happened in the short time I've been here, it's a bit overwhelming. I packed up Jessica's things last night—I couldn't stand having them in the house—and I found my grandfather's journal. I started reading it and discovered that years ago, Nigel had approached Asa about selling the plantation to your family. They had an argument, and shortly after that, my mom died, and then Cammy, a kitchen worker." I paused for a moment. "She'd been having an affair with your stepfather."

Jaxon's tanned complexion paled. "He couldn't have been married to my mom very long."

"Not long at all. I'm sorry."

He studied me closely. "That's not all, though, is it? Are you thinking he had something to do with those deaths too?"

"I don't know. It's so horrible to even think about. Like I said, everything that's gone on is overwhelming. I thought I could handle six months here, no problem, but it's been a few weeks, and I'm second-guessing my decision. Maybe you were right and I'm not cut out for this life. Maybe I really am a weak city girl."

He grabbed my shoulders. "Don't say that. You're one of the strongest people I've ever known...in this lifetime and the last." He pressed his lips to mine, caressing my mouth more than kissing it.

"I need to go back to Boston," I whispered.

He jerked back as if I'd struck him. "Are you going to leave me again?"

"There's more to it than just us."

"Like what? Last time you had no choice. You were running for your life. What are you running from now?"

I shrugged, not sure how to answer.

"You can't run from your memories, Liv. They'll hunt you down and haunt you no matter where you are, if you let them."

I knew he was right, but I still had to go. "I need to decide where I fit in. Where I call home."

"I don't like it, but I understand." When I started to walk past him, he looked over his shoulder and said, "Please, Livvy, choose me. Choose us."

Chapter Fourteen

AS THE PLANE taxied down the runway, I could barely contain my excitement at being back in Boston. And the feeling of joy only grew when I spotted my dad among the crowd of people awaiting their loved ones' arrival.

He gave me his usual bear hug, and it never felt so good. He kept the conversation light on the way to the house, and I really appreciated that. It wasn't until later, when we were relaxing in the family room, that he brought up Turnberry.

"What's going on, Liv?"

I took a moment to collect my thoughts, and then I told him all about Jessica, Nigel, and Jaxon. I even told him that I might have seen Tucker Sheldon's ghost. The only thing I didn't tell him about was my past life with Ellis. That seemed like a lot to spring on him in one night.

He regarded me quizzically for a moment. "My goodness, Liv. What a time you've had! I'm so thankful that you're okay and those dreadful people were arrested. But now they've been caught, why are you questioning whether or not to stay in Louisiana?"

I chewed on my lower lip. "Because I've fallen in love. Jaxon's wonderful. You'd like him a lot, Dad. But if I stay the full six months, how could I leave after that? It would be so much harder."

He looked confused. "If you're in love with him, Liv, why would you leave?"

I gave him a narrowed, glinting glance. "Stay in Louisiana? Forever?"

"Why not?"

My brow wrinkled. "What about you? When would I see you?"

"I'm sure you could find room in that bed-and-breakfast of yours for a visit from your father."

My breath caught in my throat. "Really? You'd come?"

"If that's where you decided to make your home, you couldn't keep me away."

"Oh, Dad." I jumped out of my chair and threw my arms around his neck. "You always make things seem so simple and clear. But I'm still not sure. I'd so been looking forward to starting my career here."

"Life has a way of throwing us all kinds of twists and turns. That's what makes it exciting."

I thought back to my journey into the past. Not too long ago, I never would have imagined anything like that was even possible. Life at Turnberry would never be boring. That was for sure.

He kissed my cheek. "Get some sleep, Livvy Luv. You've got lots to think about. Just remember, always go with your heart. If you do that, you can't go wrong."

~oɔ☉ɴℯɔɔ~

WHEN I ENTERED the Pineapple Cantina, the loud roar from the crowd of college students eating and drinking was the first thing I noticed. I'd forgotten how high the noise level could go when the place was packed.

Luckily, Kelly must've spotted me when I came in, because she was waving wildly from a booth across the room. I pushed my way through the crowd to get to her.

"Liv," she yelled, jumping up to give me a hug. "I can't believe you're back. I thought for sure you'd be gone the full six months. What's going on, girl?"

I slid into the seat across from her, glad that when I'd texted her last night asking to meet at the Pineapple today, I'd arranged for us to get here before Dale. Kelly's unique perspective on things was sure to be of help.

"So much has happened, I barely know where to begin." I leaned across the table with a big smile on my face. "I met someone, Kel."

"You did? Is it serious?"

"Yeah."

"Wow! That was fast."

"Not really, when you take into account I met him nearly two hundred years ago."

"What!" she shrieked, while practically lunging across the booth.

A waitress came by and plopped two menus down on the table.

"We're just here for drinks," Kelly said, handing them back to her. "I'll have a pineapple margarita."

"I'll have the same." When the waitress walked away, I explained, "I'm talking about past lives, reincarnation, that sort of thing."

"Olivia Lockwood! Don't tell me *you* believe in that? I predicted you'd come back believing in ghosts. I never dreamed it would go beyond that."

"I know. If you' said a few months ago that back in the 1830s, I'd been a slave at Turnberry Plantation and then escaped to Boston via the Underground Railroad, leaving behind my one true love, I'd have said you'd gone off the deep end. Yet, here I am at the Pineapple telling you that's exactly what happened."

Kelly rested her elbows on the table, her eyes as wide as saucers. "That's amazing. I'm so jealous. Tell me everything."

After revealing my entire tale to her, I'd rendered her speechless. She stared at me for a few minutes with her mouth open before managing to ask, "So if you're in love with Jaxon, does that mean you're staying in Louisiana permanently?"

Before I could answer, the waitress came by with our drinks. I took a good long sip of mine and then said, "I don't know. I don't know if I'll even stay the six months. That's why I'm here. To figure things out."

"I don't get it. What is there to figure out? You're in love with this great guy, and he loves you."

"You make it sound so simple."

"It is that simple. I don't know why you're making it difficult."

I couldn't believe my ears. "I grew up here, Kel. I never planned on leaving Boston, and then, bam, my whole world is turned upside down. My cousin tries to poison me, there's a curse on the plantation, and I find out I've lived multiple lives. That's a lot to take in."

Kelly took a drink of her margarita. "Yeah, it is. But the main thing is you've found your soul mate. Do you have any idea what I'd give to be in your shoes?"

I swallowed hard, trying to find a feeble answer. "I know I'm extremely lucky. And it's because of Jax that I might just go back to Turnberry, pack up my things, and come back here. It wouldn't be fair to stay there longer and then leave him. And right now, I'm just not ready to make that long-term commitment."

Her expression darkened. "Do you hear what

you're saying? That's exactly the excuse you used for not committing to Dale. The only difference is that you were never in love with him. You wanted that heart-pounding romance. Well, you got it, girl, and now you still can't commit. If you screw this up, Liv, I guarantee you'll spend the rest of this lifetime regretting it. Think long and hard before making a decision. And speaking of Dale, what are you going to tell him?"

I twisted my hands nervously in my lap. "Regardless of what I decide, I need to let him know that he's not the guy for me."

Kelly chugged down the rest of her drink. "You're right, so I'm going to slip out before he gets here. You know I love you. Think about what I said." She slid out of the booth, then came over to my side of the table and hugged me. "Remember, any excuse to go to Louisiana works for me, and I've always wanted to be a bridesmaid," she whispered in my ear before leaving.

I was pondering her words when Dale arrived. He looked handsome as always. "I can't believe you're here," he said, leaning over to kiss me. Although it was slow and thoughtful, it sent none of the shivers down my spine that Jaxon's kiss did.

"Yeah, it's a short visit. I'm leaving tomorrow."

He sat down across from me. "Wow! That is short. I'm glad I got to see you, though."

I forced a smile, dreading what I was going to have to tell him.

He glanced at the empty margarita glass. "Looks like Kelly came and left."

I could feel my composure starting to slip away. "Yeah... Dale you're such a good guy, and I've loved every minute I've spent with you, but..."

"But you're not in love with me."

I swallowed hard and nodded.

He reached across the table for my hand. "I know that, Liv. I just kept hoping that would change. That if I waited long enough, your feelings might match mine. But I can see that's not going to happen."

I felt impaled by his steady gaze. "You deserve someone whose eyes light up when you enter the room...who knows what you're thinking before you say it."

"Sounds like you're speaking from experience."

I took a deep breath, then let it out slowly.

There were tense lines on his face. "You don't have to answer that, Liv. It's none of my business."

"I just want you to know that this doesn't have anything to do with anyone else. We should have had this conversation a long time ago, but, like you, I kept hoping my feelings would change."

The waitress walked over and picked up the empty margarita glass. "What can I get for you?" she asked Dale.

"I'm not staying. I just popped in to say hello to a friend."

She turned to me. "Would you like the check?"

"Yes, please."

"Liv, I wish you the best. Know that I'm always there for you, if you need me. That'll never change." He got up, kissed my cheek, and then headed toward the door.

As I watched him go, tears burned beneath my lids and my throat felt tight. I was thankful he'd been so understanding and had made my telling him much easier than it might have been, but it was still painful, nonetheless.

After I paid the bill, I decided to walk home, instead of taking the T, hoping the fresh air would help clear my mind. However, when I reached my dad's house, I was still undecided about what to do.

"Hey, Dad, I'm home," I called as I opened the

front door.

He appeared at the end of the hall with his arm draped over the shoulders of a very attractive brunette. "Great timing, Liv. This is Karen, and we were just going to have some coffee. Come on in the kitchen and join us."

"Hi Livvy. It's so nice to finally get to meet you. Your dad talks about you all the time."

I smiled at my father and then Karen. "It's nice to meet you too, and I'd love a cup of coffee."

"Rough afternoon?" he asked.

I scrunched up my nose. "It's tough to say good-bye to someone you care about."

"Are you talking about Dale?"

"Yeah."

"You did the right thing, Liv."

"I know."

Karen's gaze was fixed on my dad, and the way her brown eyes sparkled, I realized she was looking at him in the way I should've looked at Dale. My heart swelled at the thought that my dad might have found what he was hoping for—a woman who could love him as much as my mom had.

I wound up having two cups of coffee while chatting and laughing with them, and for a few hours, I forgot my troubles. Unfortunately, they returned as soon as I was alone, but I didn't have to stress for long, because once my head hit the pillow, I was asleep.

THE SUN WAS barely up when we arrived at Logan. Early morning flights were always tough. However, this one was especially so. Even though I'd fallen right to sleep last night, I'd tossed and turned a lot. It seemed my dad was exhausted too. Apparently, he hadn't slept much either. For all his cheery talk the past two days, I could see how hard it was for him to say good-bye.

"I'll call you at least twice a week, Dad."

He squeezed my shoulder. "You've brought so much joy into my life, Livvy. I'm honored to be your dad. But now it's time you found your wings, kiddo. I'll support you in whatever you decide. And if it's Louisiana, I'll pack up your things and have them sent to you. You won't have to worry about a thing."

"Not all my stuff, though. I'll need some things here for when I come visit. And what about my room? Will it still be mine?"

"Livvy Luv, it'll always be yours. No matter where you go or what you do, you'll always have that to come back to."

I wrapped my arms around his neck, breathing in the aroma of his cologne. "Thanks. You're the best dad a girl could ask for. I love you so much." I clung to him a few seconds longer before kissing his cheek and saying my final good-bye.

As I walked away, I turned around once to wave. The look I saw on his face was one of deep admiration and respect, and I knew he'd meant it when he said he'd support me in whatever I decided to do.

Chapter Fifteen

THE TAXI RIDE from the airport to Turnberry was very different from the last one. Although it was another hot, muggy Louisiana day, this taxi had air-conditioning. But that wasn't the most notable difference. It was the way I felt as we approached the plantation. Last time, I'd been on pins and needles, not knowing what to expect. Now the queasy feeling in my stomach was because I had to make a life-altering decision.

When the taxi pulled up in front of the house, Gerard came and took my luggage out of the trunk and carried it inside.

"Welcome home, Miss Olivia," he said cheerfully.

"Thank you." The fact that he used the word

home struck me. I glanced around the freshly painted vestibule, noticing the new whitewashed hall table and huge vase on top of it filled with magnolias, their rich fragrance filling the room. "It looks beautiful in here. So bright and airy."

"We've all been working hard these past few days. Mr. Carter wanted everything to be perfect for when you returned."

"Well, if the rest of the house looks anything like this, I'm impressed."

"It does, Miss Olivia. I've never seen this old place look so good."

As he started up the staircase with my bags, I asked, "Speaking of Jaxon, do you happen to know where he is?"

"Last I saw, he was down by the river."

"Thanks." I walked through the vestibule and down the back hall. When I was at the kitchen, I poked my head in the door. "It's so nice to see you all looking cheerful."

Theresa, Dottie, and the rest of the staff all grinned.

"It's so nice to have ya home," Theresa said. She wiped her hands on her apron and reached for a plate of biscuits. "Would ya like somethin' to eat?

Ya must be starvin' after yar trip."

"I am. But first I need to see Jaxon. There's something I need to say to him."

She raised a brow at me but set the plate back down on the counter.

Before I left, I asked, "Have you heard from Molly?"

Dottie clapped her hands together. "She's comin' home tomorrow. Words can't express how grateful I am that she's well."

"It is indeed something to be very thankful for. Be sure to make a special dinner tomorrow, ladies."

"Oh, we will, Miss Olivia. We most certainly will, and with one of my fabulous puddin' cakes for dessert," Theresa added.

As I walked out the back door onto the rear porch, it struck me how often *home* had been mentioned in the span of a few minutes. I wandered through the French parterre garden, taking in how precisely it had been pruned. When I passed through the white swinging gates and then over to the back buildings—the pigeonnier, the sugar house, and the slave quarters—it was as if I'd gone back more than a century. Every last detail had been attended to. My chest filled with pride that a little piece of history had been restored and would soon be shared with the public.

I continued on to where the cypress trees with their branches dripping with Spanish moss framed the Mississippi. A heron walked leisurely over the grass, until its keen eyes spotted me. It opened its beautiful wings and took off in graceful flight.

At the edge of the riverbank, I spotted Jaxon. As if sensing I was there, he turned around to face me. "I didn't expect you until later."

"I got an early flight," I said, standing beside him.

There were shadows under his eyes and a tenseness to his mouth.

"The place looks wonderful." I offered him a smile, hoping to lighten the mood, but he didn't return the gesture.

"Did you hear Molly's coming home tomorrow?"

"Yes, Dottie told me. That was the news I was hoping to hear." I put my hand on his arm. "Jaxon, I—"

"You were right about everything, Liv," he said cutting me off. "I found out a little while ago that Nigel confessed. He used that kitchen worker

Cammy to put arsenic in your mom's sweet tea, and then he killed her. He thought that with your mom out of the way, Asa would sell Turnberry. When that didn't happen, he just bided his time until the next opportunity presented itself. That happened to be Jess. He thought he'd found his golden goose, but that changed when you came on the scene. He had to get you out of the way, so he resorted to what worked in the past—murder with arsenic. Molly was a diversion, and the Tucker Sheldon curse played right into his hands. And then there was Asa..."

I breathed in a shallow, quick gasp. "Grandpa?"

"That last night, Jess poisoned his soup."

I squeezed my eyes shut, trying to block out the image of my grandfather's still body.

"He was dying, Liv. They just helped it along," he said bitterly. "All this tragedy because a petrochemical company offered to buy Clairmont, but for the deal to go through, they wanted Turnberry too." He looked back over the water. "I'm so sorry. I had no idea Nigel was so twisted."

"You can't blame yourself, Jaxon. How could you have known? You were just a boy when he started down his sick path."

"I wouldn't blame you if you turned around

and went right back to Boston."

My back stiffened. "Why would I do that?"

"So much has happened here, why would you want to stay?"

"Didn't you say, 'You can't run from your memories? They'll hunt you down and haunt you no matter where you are, if you let them'? And what about the grand opening of the bed-and-breakfast? All the work that you and everyone here has done to get this place ready would've all been for nothing."

"Not for nothing. If you leave, Turnberry goes to the historical society. I'm sure they'd be very happy to get this place fully renovated."

"But this is my home."

There was a pensive shimmer in the shadow of his eyes. "A home that's cursed."

"A curse is only effective if you let it be. Our love is stronger than any hex from Tucker Sheldon."

His face brightened. "You mean that?"

I curled my arms around his neck, pulling him to me. "I choose you. I choose us. Now and forever." My mouth covered his hungrily, and when he kissed me back, it was with a savage intensity that rocked my world.

I had no doubt I'd made the right choice. After

all, I'd followed my dad's advice: always go with your heart. If you do that, you can't go wrong.

The End

About the Author

USA TODAY bestselling author Raine English began her career as a journalist, but writing romance novels was her passion. Her books have won many awards, including finalling in the Romance Writers of America® Golden Heart® and winning the Daphne du Maurier Award.

When not behind her computer, you can find her reading, usually something involving the supernatural. She lives in New England with her family and two French bulldogs, Dolly and Bailey.

Visit Raine's website
www.RaineEnglish.com

Join Raine on Facebook
www.facebook.com/RaineEnglish

Follow Raine on Twitter
www.twitter.com/RaineEnglish

www.ingramcontent.com/pod-product-compliance
Lightning Source LLC
Chambersburg PA
CBHW022120170626
46808CB00002B/786